Cathy Hopkins

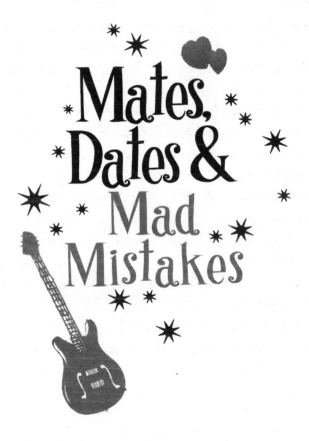

Mates,
Dates &
Mad
Mistakes

PICCADILLY PRESS • LONDON

*Thanks as always to Brenda Gardner, Yasemin Uçar and the team at
Piccadilly for making working on these books such a pleasure.
To Rosemary Bromley at Juvenelia for all her support. To Steve
Lovering for all his help and for being a great sounding board. And
to Rachel Hopkins, Georgina Acar, Scott Brenman, Becca Crewe,
Alice Elwes, Jenni Herzberg, Olivia McDonnell and Annie McGrath
for keeping in touch with me on e-mail about what's what with
teenagers and for answering all my questions.*

First published in Great Britain in 2003
by Piccadilly Press Ltd.,
5 Castle Road, London NW1 8PR
This edition published 2007

A catalogue record for this book is available from
the British Library

ISBN: 978 1 85340 932 5 (trade paperback)

3 5 7 9 10 8 6 4 2

Printed in the UK by CPI Bookmarque, Croydon, CR0 4TD

Chapter 1

Chickens

'Sounds horrible,' said Nesta, pulling a face.

'What?' I asked as Lucy and I came back into her bedroom with sleepover supplies (the usual: Diet Cokes, Salt & Vinegar Pringles and Liquorice Allsorts). TJ, Nesta and I were staying over at Lucy's, after she'd held a girls-only party earlier in the evening. We'd finished clearing up after the other girls had left and were ready for some late night nattering before getting into our sleeping bags.

'Yeah, what sounds horrible?' asked Lucy.

TJ pointed to a book of spells that I'd lent Lucy earlier in the summer. 'Becoming blood sisters,' said TJ in a spooky voice. 'Says in Izzie's book that if you want to bond with your mates for life, the best way to do it is to each prick your finger with a needle, then press the tiny

'Yee-*uck*,' said Nesta. 'Can't we burn our bras instead, like those women in the sixties?'

Lucy laughed. 'No we can't, because seeing as I have no chest to speak of, I haven't got a bra to burn.'

'Yes you have,' said Nesta. 'I've seen it.'

Lucy shook her head. 'I chucked it out. No point. It was after something Lal said. He asked, if I had no feet would I still wear shoes? I said no, course not. So then he said, so why do you wear a bra?'

'What a cheek. What does he know?' I said as I put down the Pringles. 'That's really mean, even for a brother.'

Lucy shrugged. 'Nah, he's right. I only wore one because everyone else does. For show. Trouble was, nothing *did* show except an empty wrinkle of lacy fabric under my T-shirt. It's much more comfortable without one.'

'Oh, let's do the blood sister thing,' said TJ. 'It'll be a laugh and we'll be friends for ever and ever.'

I shook my head. 'Nah, sounds daft. It's the sort of thing that kids do, junior school stuff . . .'

'And this coming from Mystic Iz, Queen of Witchiness herself,' said TJ. 'What's up with you?'

I shrugged. 'Nothing. It just sounds childish. I've had that spell book for years. I read it when I was in Year *Seven*.'

TJ looked disappointed. 'I think it sounds cool. And

there's a nice sentiment behind it – makes a change from all those spells you usually do for getting boys and stuff.'

'Yeah, let's try it,' said Lucy.

'Well, you have to sterilise the needles, you know,' said Nesta.

Lucy rolled her eyes. 'You're such a prissy-knickers.'

'No, actually she's right,' said TJ. 'Best be on the safe side.'

'Yes, better had, Lucy,' I said. TJ's parents are both doctors so if anyone should know about what's safe and what's not, it's them.'

'Oh, all right,' said Lucy. 'I will.'

'And as long as it won't hurt . . .' said Nesta.

'It won't,' said Lucy as she began to look for needles in her sewing box. She found a sachet of them and waved them in the air. 'Won't be a mo. I'll just put on my nurse's uniform and go and sterilise these.'

She was back a few minutes later and handed us a needle each.

'If we're going to do this, let's do it properly,' I said. 'We should sit in a circle, and Lucy, can we light a candle?'

'Ah, so Mystic Iz isn't quite dead, then?' said Nesta, grinning.

Lucy found a candle, lit it, then turned off the electric light and we sat in a circle on the floor.

Lucy, TJ and I did it straight away. A quick jab and we were ready.

Nesta screwed her face up and put the needle close to her thumb, like she was trying to puncture the skin really slowly. 'I can't,' she moaned. 'I really can't. I hate needles and it's going to *hurt*.'

'Just do it quickly,' said Lucy. 'It just takes a second and only feels like . . . like a quick prick.'

'I could answer that with something very rude,' laughed Nesta. 'But I won't. Are you *sure* these needles are sterilised properly, Luce? We might get some horrible disease. I don't think it's safe to share blood.'

'Chicken,' I said.

'Oh, come on you big sissy,' said TJ, taking the needle from her. 'I'll do it for you.'

'No, *no*,' she cried, rolling over on the floor on top of her hands. 'You'll stab me or hit an artery or something.'

'Trust me, I'm a doctor,' said TJ. 'Or at least my parents are.'

'No,' said Nesta, getting up again. 'I'll do it myself.' Once again, she softly prodded her thumb with the needle. 'No . . . It's not working. No. Sorry. Can't do it.'

'Well, we can't carry on if you don't,' said Lucy. 'It wouldn't be right. Me, TJ and Izzie would be bonded for life and you'd be on the outside. It might be awful bad luck.'

'Yeah, come on, cowardy custard,' I said, massaging my thumb. 'My blood's drying up.'

'I'm sorry, I can't. I just can't.' Nesta leaned back and grabbed the spell book off the bed. 'Isn't there some other thing we can do to bond us for life? Something that doesn't involve *pain*?' She reached for the Pringles. 'How about we all take a bite of one of these and pass it on. Bond over a Pringle. Same sort of thing – caring sharing, bonding schmonding.'

I had to laugh. Nesta never takes anything like doing spells seriously. 'Go on, then, pass us a Pringle,' I said.

Nesta selected one from the tub, then we passed it around, each taking a tiny bite of it.

'OK, by the power vested in me by this salt and vinegar crisp,' I said in my best solemn voice, 'I hereby decree that these four girls gathered here tonight shall be friends for ever and ever, bound together by the magical force of the Almighty Pringle.'

Lucy and Nesta started laughing. 'All hail to the Pringle,' said Lucy.

'All hail,' echoed TJ and I.

Then I had an idea. 'OK, then how about this? If we really want to have an experience that will bond us, how about doing something that will look good as well?'

'What do you mean?' asked TJ. 'Like dressing up to do spells?'

'No. How about we get our belly buttons pierced?'

There was a stunned silence. I don't think they expected anything like that, but I'd been thinking about having it done for a while. Part of a whole new image. We were going into Year Ten at school a week on

Monday and somehow I wanted to leave the old Izzie behind with the old year. I felt like I'd grown out of so many of the things I'd been into, including my clothes – literally, with some of them. I seemed to have shot up a few more inches over the last year and some of my jeans were stopping short of my ankles. *Très* uncool. Anyway, I'd told Mum that I was having a mid-teen crisis and needed some new clothes. She'd laughed and said there was no such thing as a *mid*-teen crisis, as when you're a teen, it's crisis all the way through – mainly for her. Poo. I don't think she knows how lucky she is. If she knew what some of the girls at our school get up to behind their parents' backs, she'd have a fit. Relatively, I give her an easy time, although *she* doesn't think so.

'Hmm,' said Nesta finally. 'Having a stud put in will probably hurt as well, won't it? But . . . I *have* always wanted one.' She stroked her impossibly flat tummy. 'Yeah, a belly button stud would look neat.'

'It won't hurt,' I said. 'Candice Carter had hers done. She was telling me earlier this evening at the party. She said they put stuff on your tummy that kind of freezes it so you don't feel anything.'

'Well, I'm in,' said Lucy. 'I need all the help I can get, to get boys to notice me. A belly button stud would look really cool and might detract from the fact that I have no basoomas.'

'Basoomas?' asked TJ. 'What are they?'

Lucy pointed at her chest. 'Boobs, you idiot. Lal calls them basoomas or jaloobis.'

TJ pulled a face. 'He needs help, does your brother.'

'Tell me about it,' sighed Lucy.

'We could all have a different colour stone on our stud,' I said. 'Have you got any books on astrology, Lucy?'

'Course,' she said, getting up and going to her shelf. 'That one you gave me last Christmas.'

When she handed me the book, I had a quick flick through and found a section on which stones and colours are right for different signs. 'OK, here it is, our birthstones. It says garnet for those born in January, so that's me.'

'What colour is a garnet?' asked Lucy.

'Sort of deep wine red,' I answered.

Lucy nodded approvingly. 'That would look good on you with your dark hair.'

'Nesta, you're Leo,' I continued, 'so it says . . . Let me see . . . Oh, it could be a diamond or a ruby. Wow, that would look fab against your dark skin. Really exotic.'

'Nah,' said Nesta shaking her head. 'I'd look like some belly dancer. No. I want a diamond if I'm going to have anything. Much classier.'

'Fine, whatever,' I said. 'Lucy, Gemini, born May 24th . . . it says emerald for you.'

'An emerald might look better on you, Izzie,' said Nesta, 'to go with your green eyes.'

'Yeah. I'd rather have a sapphire,' said Lucy. 'You know, blue, to match *my* eyes.'

'Yeah, and blue suits blondes,' said Nesta.

'Well, we don't *have* to stick to this,' I said. 'It's just if we wanted our birthstones.'

'What's mine?' asked TJ.

I flicked through the book to Sagittarius. 'OK, November to December. It says November, topaz, December, turquoise. You were born November 24th, so topaz. It'd be great.'

'Topaz? That's yellow, isn't it?' asked TJ. 'I don't think that's a good colour for a belly button stud at all. You know how some of them go a bit ucky – a yellow stone might look like a lump of solid puss or something.'

'Er *TJ, g-ross,*' laughed Nesta. 'But I think you're right. I think a turquoise would look better on a brunette like you.'

I closed the book, put the back of my hand on my forehead and sighed my best tragic sigh. 'I despair. Sometimes I wonder why I *bother* with you ignoramuses. I just thought we could be the Birthstone Belly Button Gang, that's all.'

'You're mad, Izzie,' laughed Lucy. 'But it would be nice if we all got different colours.'

TJ was looking dubious. 'I don't know. You lot have all got really flat tummies but mine's rounded. I don't think they look as good if your stomach isn't like a washboard.

Besides, won't it cost a fortune? I don't think I'll have enough, with the pocket money I get.'

'Good point,' said Lucy. 'Cost – what do you think?'

'I'll find out,' I said. 'I doubt it will be that much. I mean, it's not like we're buying real diamonds and gold or anything.'

TJ still looked anxious. 'I don't think my mum and dad will like it.'

'They don't need to see it,' said Nesta. 'We're going back to school in just over a week. Soon we'll be in winter clothes. No one will see it.'

'So what's the point of having one done?' asked TJ.

'When we're out together, stupoid,' said Nesta. 'When we wear crop tops.'

'I guess,' said TJ.

'So we all in?' I asked.

The others nodded, TJ somewhat reluctantly.

'Right then,' I said. 'Tomorrow morning. I've seen a place in Kentish Town near where the band plays. We'll go there.'

Birthstones

January: Garnet (wine red)
February: Amethyst (purple/violet)
March: Aquamarine (bluish green)
April: Diamond (clear)
May: Emerald (green)
June: Pearl (off-white)
July: Ruby (red)
August: Peridot (olive green)
September: Sapphire (bright blue)
October: Opal (milk white)
November: Topaz (yellow gold)
December: Turquoise (turquoise)

This can differ to starsigns, and according to what book or website you use.

Chapter 2

No Pain, No Gain

TJ was the first to cop out.

'I can't,' she said as we stood in front of a tattoo shop in
Kentish Town on Saturday morning, trying to summon up
the courage to go in. I had half a mind to agree with her
and call the whole thing off. It was one thing having an
idea, it was another actually carrying it through, and I was
feeling distinctly nervous. It will be OK, I told myself as I
glanced at a couple of guys leaning against the shop front
smoking cigarettes. Both were a bit hard-looking, dressed
in Camden black, and I wondered if they were the ones
who did the piercing or just customers hanging out. Either
way, both of them were walking advertisements for the
shop. Their arms were completely covered in tattoos and
they had studs everywhere, in their noses, in their lips . . .

and one had little pointy studs on top of his ears that made him look like Mr Spock in *Star Trek*.

'I'm really sorry,' continued TJ, 'but Mum and Dad would kill me. I know we agreed not to tell our parents, but . . . I can't risk it. You know what my dad's like.'

We all nodded. Everyone calls TJ's dad Scary Dad. He's a lot older than the rest of our dads and is very strict and solemn-looking. I'd probably cop out as well if he was my father.

'Plus,' said TJ, 'we don't know how much it costs yet and I've already spent most of this month's pocket money. Mum and Dad would get suspicious if I asked them for any more, you know. They'd want to know what I'd spent my money on.'

'No worries, TJ. Me and Nesta will go in and check it out,' I said. 'Get the details and find out if it's all cool. If it looks remotely dodgy, we don't do it. OK?'

'It *will* be OK,' said Lucy as Nesta and I headed for the door.

As we approached, one of the guys with a goatee smiled at us. 'Can I help you, ladies?' he asked.

'Um, yes,' I said. 'We wanted to ask about piercings.'

'Then come this way,' he said and led us into the shop. Inside, it looked normal enough – very clean, with posters on sale and jewellery on display. At the back were what looked like hairdressing chairs in front of mirrors, and I could see what looked like a dentist's chair in a room off to the right. A shiver went down my spine.

'So what do you want to know?' asked Goatee Man.

'How much is it to have your belly button pierced?' said Nesta.

'Thirty-five pounds,' he said. 'Is it for you?'

We both nodded.

'How old are you?'

'Sixteen,' Nesta lied.

The man shook his head. 'Then you'd have to come with your parents. We don't do belly button piercings without parental consent. Sorry.'

'But we *do* have our parents' consent,' I fibbed. 'They're totally cool about it.' Haha. Big lie. My mum would hit the roof if she knew where I was, but I didn't think it would be a problem. She wouldn't even notice. She never pays much attention to me these days, except to lecture me about where I've been and what time I get back.

Goatee Man grinned. 'That's what they all say, darlin'. Nice try, but sorry, no go.'

Nesta and I went back out to join TJ and Lucy. 'No go,' said Nesta. 'We need our parents' permission.'

TJ looked relieved, but Lucy looked disappointed.

'And it's thirty-five pounds,' I said.

'That's me definitely out, then,' said TJ. 'I've only got fifteen pounds fifty.'

'Maybe they'd do a deal and put it halfway in,' laughed Lucy.

TJ punched her arm. 'Haha. But have you got enough?'

'I've got forty quid that my gran sent me for my birthday,' said Nesta. 'I could lend someone five.'

'I've got thirty,' said Lucy. 'That's all my savings.'

'I'll lend you the last five,' said Nesta. 'What about you, Iz?'

'I've just got it. Dad gave me twenty quid a few weeks ago and I saved it. With what's left of my pocket money from Mum, I could just about do it.'

TJ pointed back at the shop. 'But they said they wouldn't do it without permission.'

'We could go somewhere else,' said Nesta, 'and blag our way in. You know, slap a bit of make-up on and say we're eighteen.'

Lucy's face fell even further. 'Yeah right. Like anyone's ever going to believe that I'm eighteen. It's OK for you lot. You're all tall and look older, but me . . . I'm minuscule and look younger than I am. It's not fair.'

'Don't worry, Luce, we'll think of something,' said Nesta. 'We won't do it without you.'

'Let's phone Candice,' said Lucy. 'No way she had *her* parents' permission if I know her. I'm going to find out where she got hers done.' She punched Candice's number in on her mobile and wandered off down the street to talk to her. A few minutes later, she was back smiling. 'Candice says that there are loads of places in Camden that will do them. She says some of them won't and get all snotty about your age, but to keep trying as there are a few where there are no questions asked. She gave me directions to the one she went to.'

'Let's go,' I said. Now that we had started on Mission Belly Stud, I wanted to get it over with. Although I was brave about the thumb pricking, really I'm a bit like Nesta in that I don't like needles. I'd had a sleepless night thinking about what having the stud might feel like when it was being put in and I'd had weird dreams about giant needles chasing me.

Twenty minutes later, we found the shop that Candice had told Lucy about. Although it sold mainly clothes, belts and boots, there was a discreet sign on the till saying 'Body Piercing' and pointing to the back of the shop. A shop assistant at the counter nodded towards a door when she saw us looking at the sign. So far, so good, I thought. I knocked on the door, but there was no answer.

'Just go on in,' said the assistant. 'Del's in there some-where.'

I opened the door and we all trooped in. The first thing that hit me was an overpowering smell of antiseptic. There was a small reception room with the usual display of studs and rings and a door to the left, which was ajar. Through it, I could see and *hear* a man having a tattoo done on his upper arm. He didn't look like he was enjoying it one bit and looked out at us with thin tight lips.

The man doing the tattoo glanced up at us. 'Won't be a mo, girls. Take a seat.'

We dutifully sat down and looked around. 'This is like waiting to see the dentist,' said Nesta. 'It even *sounds* like a dentist's with that tattoo thing buzzing. I feel really nervous.'

'It's going to be well worth it,' said Lucy. 'We're going to look so glam.'

'So who's going first?' I said. 'We'd better decide.'

'I will,' said Lucy. 'I hate waiting and I want to get it over with.'

'Do you want to go next, Nesta?' I asked.

She shook her head. 'No hurry. I don't mind waiting. I need to gear myself up mentally.'

'I'll go second,' I said. 'That way you'll know it's all right.'

'OK,' said Nesta. 'Thanks.'

A few minutes later, the tattooist and his 'victim' came out. Interesting, I thought, because the tattooist didn't have any tattoos, or at least none that were visible. He looked very ordinary, in fact. He was wearing a normal shirt and trousers – not at all like the typical Camden characters who wear black or Goth clothes. On the other hand, the victim was covered in tattoos. He had a shaved head and swirly patterns all over his arms and up his neck. He looks weird, I thought, like he belongs in the circus or something. Then I realised that I was staring at him and quickly looked at the floor.

'Right, I'm Del,' said the tattooist after Circus Boy had gone. 'What is it you're after?'

'Piercing,' said Lucy.

'Ears, eyebrows, nose, lips, tongues, belly or nipples?' asked Del.

Lucy went bright red. 'Um, belly buttons.'

'All of you?'

Lucy looked back at TJ. 'All of us?'

'It'll be thirty pounds each,' said the tattooist.

'That means Lucy's got enough,' said Nesta, 'so I can lend you a ten, TJ. Then I could ask my brother – he always seems to have loads of dosh. I can call him on my mobile and ask if he'll bring the rest if you want. I'm sure he'd come, especially if I tell him Lucy's here.'

Predictably, Lucy blushed again. She always does when anyone mentions Tony, even though it's him that's running after her these days, not the other way around.

TJ shook her head. 'No. You guys go ahead. I'd be too worried about my dad ever finding out. Anyway, we've bonded over the Almighty Pringle and that's good enough for me.'

'All hail,' chorused Nesta and Lucy. The tattooist looked amused.

'You sure?' I said to TJ.

TJ nodded, so I turned back to the tattooist. 'Three of us

for belly buttons,' I said, then I got an attack of the giggles at the thought of us getting our nipples pierced. I imagined going home and flashing my chest at Mum over dinner. Whoa! Look what I've had done, Mater. She'd go *ballistic*. But no worries. I mean, really, who in their right mind would ever want to have a nipple pierced? Yee–*uck*.

'Who's first?' said Del.

Well, that was easy, I thought, as Lucy stepped forward and Del ushered her into his work room. We watched from the reception room as she lay on the chair, then I couldn't see any more because Del's back was in my way.

It didn't seem to take long. She was out a short time later and took a huge breath. 'Not too bad. Like having your ears done,' she said giving me the thumbs–up. 'Not as bad as I thought.'

'Next,' called Del.

I got up and felt my knees go wobbly. Was it too late to do a runner? Whose stupid idea was this? I asked myself. Oh yeah. Mine! No. No, I can do this.

'Can I come in and watch?' asked Nesta as I went in. 'I want to know what I'm letting myself in for.'

'Sure,' said Del. 'You can all come in if you want.'

'Er, no thanks,' said TJ. 'I'll stay here with Lucy.'

I lay back on the chair and closed my eyes. Then I opened them. Del was coming at me with a pair of weird–looking scissors. They looked distorted like something out of a horror film.

'What are *they* for?' I asked in a panic. 'You're not going to cut your way through, are you?'

Del smiled. 'Nah, mate. These are to clamp your tummy. They make the skin go nice and tight.'

Next thing I knew, he'd fastened the strange-looking scissors to the skin above my belly button and was wiping the area with some kind of lotion. I felt like I was going to pass out, it smelt so like a hospital.

'Is that the stuff to freeze it?' I asked.

'No,' said Del. 'It's antiseptic. Keeps the area clean. I don't freeze the skin, though my partner does. We've all got our own way, but too risky, I reckon – you might get frostbite. Don't worry, it will only sting for a minute.'

I closed my eyes and opened them again. He was taking something out of a small plastic sachet. It looked like a minuscule screwdriver. 'That's not the needle, is it?' I asked. 'It's *enormous*.'

'Just take a deep breath,' he said. 'You've got to suffer to be beautiful, right? No pain, no gain.'

I closed my eyes again and desperately searched my mind for one of the soothing visualisations I use to take my mind off the discomfort when I go to the dentist's. Sea, waves, nice flowers, I thought, as I felt a searing pain rip through my middle. 'Whara . . . *arghhhhhhh*,' I cried.

'All done.' Del smiled, taking out a plaster and putting it over my belly button. 'You can get up now. Now that wasn't so bad, was it?'

'Urg,' was all I could say as I stumbled out of the chair.

Nesta had turned pale and backed out of the room. 'Er, thanks,' she whispered, 'but . . . but I think I might wait until another day.'

'Nihi – ergh,' said TJ and ran out the reception door and into the shop with Nesta.

I felt faint. I just wanted to get out of there, but Del insisted on sitting Lucy and me down and giving us a *looong* lecture on how to clean the stud and the importance of being hygienic.

'And don't take the stud out for four to six weeks,' he said. 'Couple of months, if possible. I'm serious now, as you need to give the area time to heal. I know you girls are always anxious to get the pretty stones in, but start messing about with it before it's completely healed and it can get really ucky.' Then he handed us each a bottle of cleansing lotion. 'Salt water,' he said. 'Use it to clean the area three times a day, and mind you don't let the stud catch in your clothes in the early days.'

I nodded like I'd understood, but I don't think I took in anything he said. I felt strangely floaty, as though I wasn't quite present any more.

We paid our money and at last we were out of there. I gulped the air when we got out into the street and Lucy put her arm under mine to steady me. 'You OK?' she asked.

'Heh-nuh . . .' I said.

Lucy grinned. 'I didn't think it was bad at all.'

I guess she has a higher pain threshold than I do. I thought it was *awful*. And to think, I'd *paid* to have it done.

'Drinks are on me,' said Nesta as we headed up to Chalk Farm. 'I feel rotten that I chickened out, but . . .'

'Hey, no biggie,' I said. 'I'd have done the same if I'd known what it entailed.'

'Are you OK now?' asked Lucy.

I nodded. 'Just needed some fresh air. To get away from the smell of antiseptic. I know it's supposed to be good, but I always associate it with sickness and it makes me feel nauseous.'

'So let's head over to Primrose Hill Park. Lots of air up there,' said TJ, who up until now had kept very quiet. I guess she was feeling bad about chickening out as well.

When we got to the park, TJ and Nesta shot off to get drinks from the nearby shops and Lucy and I sat on the grass halfway up the hill.

'How long do you think we can spin this out?' asked Lucy with a wicked grin as she watched them go. 'They are both obviously prepared to be our slaves because they feel bad.'

I grinned back. 'As long as possible, then. Every time we need something done, we can flash our belly buttons at them and groan.'

We lay on the grass and practised our groaning for a while until a man walking his dog stopped and asked if we were all right.

Lucy went bright red. 'Um, yeah, just something we ate for lunch.'

Luckily he moved on, so I sat up and looked about the park. It felt really calm. The only sound was the hum of distant traffic. There were the usual people out enjoying the late August sun – mums with toddlers, a few joggers, a guy on a bench listening to his iPod and a number of teens hanging out farther down the hill.

Suddenly, the roar of a motorbike shattered the peace as it zoomed down the hill to our left. I glanced through the railings to see who it was – some guy wearing black leather trousers and a tight black T-shirt.

'*Eejit*,' said Lucy. 'I *hate* those things. They're so *noisy*.'

'Yeah, but I'd quite like a go on the back of one of them. Wouldn't you?'

Lucy shook her head. 'Nah. Think I'll stick with my limo fantasy, thank you very much.'

As Nesta and TJ returned laden with drinks and pastries about ten minutes later, I noticed that the motorbike guy came into the park behind them and went to join the other group of teens down the hill.

'Don't like the look of that lot,' said TJ, glancing at them as she sat down.

They didn't look much older than us, maybe sixteen or so. Six of them. I counted. Three boys and three girls. A few of them were smoking, and a few were sharing cans of what looked like beer. One of the boys started acting stupid, throwing things around. It was funny because he was clearly trying to impress Bike Boy. When Bike Boy didn't react, he started throwing bits of sandwich at a jogger who was running past. Still no reaction. Well, you can see who's king of the castle there, I thought. Bike Boy got up and went to stand a short distance apart from the rest of them. He leaned back against the railings, lit up a cigarette and glanced around the park. As he looked up at us, I felt a rush go through me. There was something about him. Tall, dark, slim and looks like he works out, I thought. He had well-toned arms – not big muscles, just nicely shaped.

'Bad boy, but very cute,' said Nesta, casually glancing around the park and noticing that I'd clocked him. I laughed. She doesn't miss a trick.

Lucy looked over to him. 'Yeah, handsome, but he looks dangerous.'

'Never judge a book by its cover,' I said. 'Like that guy in the first tattoo shop – he looked hard, but he was a real sweetie when we got talking to him.'

'I guess with boys it depends on what you're looking for,' said TJ. 'I think it's important to find a boy who's dependable.'

'Yeah, but fun,' I said.

'And a good kisser,' said Nesta. 'Very important.'

Lucy rubbed her forehead. 'Hmmm. I know a joke about finding the perfect boy – if only I could remember it . . .'

'Well, he doesn't look like the perfect boy,' said TJ, looking at Bike Boy. 'He looks like trouble and boys that good-looking are usually self-obsessed.'

I looked at him again. I wouldn't say that, I thought. I think he looks like he knows how to have a good time. Then I realised that we were all gawping at him. How uncool is that?

'Stop looking, *stop looking*,' I whispered to the others. 'He can see we're staring.'

Too late. He'd already noticed. He raised an eyebrow and gave us a lazy smile before going back to his mates. Then he flopped down next to one of the boys and said something into his ear. They both turned, looked at us and laughed. He probably thinks we're a bunch of kids, I thought, as I sipped on the Ribena Lite that Nesta had bought me. I pretended that I was laughing at something Lucy had said, then I purposefully looked straight at him then in the opposite direction. Two can play at that game, matie, I thought.

Lucy's Joke

It's important to find a boy who is always willing to help in times of trouble.

It's important to find a boy who makes you laugh when you're feeling blue.

It's important to find a boy who is dependable and doesn't lie.

It's important to find a boy who is a good kisser.

It's important these four boys never meet.

Chapter 3

Restyle

'How's the stud?' I whispered to Lucy the next morning as I let her in the front door.

'Fine,' she said and followed me up the stairs. 'Yours?'

I pulled a face. 'Gone a bit crusty, if you must know, and it stings like anything when I put that salt water on it.'

'Mine's been OK,' said Lucy as we went into my bedroom and I shut the door. 'But I showed Mum and Dad, I'm afraid. I couldn't resist.'

'And?'

'Dad hit the roof for a while and Mum was miffed that I hadn't asked permission, but they were both cool in the end. In fact, Mum came into my room last night and asked where I'd had it done.'

'Why? She's not going to go and hassle them, is she? About us being under-age?'

'Nah. She said *she* wanted one!'

'No!'

'That's what I said. I said if she dared to have her belly button pierced, I'd leave home.'

'Quite right,' I said. 'Yuck. I can't imagine my mum ever having one done. The thought is too disgusting.' And totally unlikely, I thought. She likes the classic look and is always immaculate in beige or black. The only earrings she ever wears are little pearl studs.

Lucy shivered. 'Yeah, image overload. Let's change the subject. So . . .' She looked around my room, taking in the piles of clothes I'd thrown on the bed, chair and floor.

'I know,' I said. 'I pulled out everything. I want to do a real throw-out. I've found stuff in my drawers that I've had for years.'

'OK,' said Lucy and began to sort through things. 'We'll make two piles, one for the bin, one for keeping.' She picked up a pink vest. 'Oh, you must keep this. It's really pretty.'

'Nooo. It's too . . . boring.'

Lucy moved some clothes aside and sat on my bed. 'Well what image exactly are you going for?'

I sat next to her. 'Dunno. That's why you're here, style queen.'

Lucy's been my closest friend for ages and I really trust her opinion. Not that I don't trust TJ and Nesta, I do, but I've know Lucy longer – since junior school – and we've shared everything from clothes and CDs to our first day at secondary school. Sometimes we even know what each other is thinking. Also, she's great on fashion. She makes loads of her own clothes and wants to study dress design after secondary school. That's why I asked her rather than Nesta or TJ to help me go through my wardrobe. It's not that Nesta hasn't got style, she has. But if she had her way, she'd dress everyone like her, in girlie clothes, and what suits her doesn't necessarily suit everyone. I'm not a girlie type of girl. And TJ's the opposite of Nesta. She's a bit of a tomboy. She does look good in her jeans and trainers, but she's not that bothered about clothes really. She'd rather spend her pocket money on a book than a top.

'All I know is I need a change,' I said. 'Something more sophisticated, something to make me stand out. Like, I know I'll never be drop-dead gorgeous like Nesta . . .'

'Rubbish,' interrupted Lucy. 'You have a different look, that's all, but you're just as good-looking as she is.'

Typical Lucy. Always my champion.

'Get real,' I said. 'I know where I stand in the beauty stakes, and Nesta is a nine and a half out of ten . . . and I'm about a five without any make-up, but can be a seven or eight if I make a bit of an effort. Fact. Reality.'

'You're too critical of yourself. I'd give you a nine, easy. You've got a great figure, fabulous eyes, lovely hair . . .'

'Thank you very much, Lucy,' I said, 'but sorry, I don't

share your view. My bum's too big for a start and my nose is too lumpy.'

'I saw a programme on telly about model school and one of the first things they teach is about confidence. The girls have to do an exercise where they go up to mirrors and tell themselves that they're beautiful. Makes sense, because if you don't believe it, no one else will. If you think you're a five, Izzie, that's what you put out to people. You of all people should know that.'

I got up and stood in front of the mirror on my bedroom door. 'You are beautiful. You are beeeoootiful,' I told myself, then laughed. 'No, I'm not. I can look interesting, or maybe attractive, but I know I'll never be beautiful.'

Lucy threw a pillow at me. 'You're blind, Iz.'

'Don't worry,' I said. 'I'm not major freaked about it, I'm being honest, that's all. I really don't mind if you are too. I think we all should be. Us girls, we're all afraid to say anything critical. In reality, everyone knows exactly what their assets and flaws are.'

Lucy sighed. 'OK, you're an ugly old bag.'

'I know I'm not that either, but I reckon that if you want to get noticed, there are three ways – you're either drop-dead gorgeous to begin with, like Nesta, who would look fab in a bin bag. Or you develop your own style – one that stands out from the crowd. You know, wild clothes or something. Or third, you wear clothes that are provocative. Cool, alluring. The worst thing is to be boring.'

'No one could ever say you're boring, Iz.'

I chucked a pair of baggy trousers on the 'bin' pile. 'Well, that's just it. I seem to go from mad clothes that are definitely different, to boring clothes that make me look invisible. I want to find a new look, one that really suits me.'

'OK then, but it's not just clothes,' said Lucy. 'Someone can wear the most fab designer labels and still look crapola. Like Linda Parker in Year Eleven. I saw her at the cinema the other week and she was showing off in some Dolce and Gabbana number, but a) just because her stuff was by a posh designer doesn't mean it suited her, and b) her posture is crap. That's the other thing that they teach at model school: walk tall, don't slouch. And of course we all know that someone can be beautiful on the outside, but boring as anything inside.'

I laughed. 'You sound like a magazine article.'

'Actually, TJ asked me to do one for the school magazine,' she admitted. 'She's been working on ideas over the holidays for the autumn edition. I've been doing top tips for making the most of yourself, so I've been thinking a lot about it. In the end, though, it's personality that makes you want to be with people. I hang out with Nesta because she's a laugh and big-hearted, not because she looks good.'

'True,' I said. 'But try telling a gorgeous boy all that

stuff about how much personality matters. I read in one of my mags that boys are ninety-five percent visual. The first thing they notice is what girls look like – hair, shape, legs and so on. With girls, looks are important too, but to a lesser degree. You've got to make boys notice you in the first place so that they'll take the time to get to know your personality.'

'Ben seemed to like you the way you were.'

Ben was my boyfriend until last week. He plays in the band that I sing with and we'll still be mates, I hope.

'Yeah, he liked me the way I was. But I want to change. Finishing with him was part of it. I mean, we got on and everything, but it all started to feel too safe, predictable. All we ever did was band stuff. I feel like I've spent the whole of the holidays stuck in his garage going over songs, and although I know you have to practise if you want to be good, I want a bit more excitement. It's like, I dunno, Ben doesn't have any edge. Not a great challenge any more.'

'So you want a new image to get a new boy?'

'Not necessarily just to get a boy. It's part of it. It's just that, I dunno . . . I feel different lately. I want my clothes to reflect that. I want to do cool, sophisticated, a bit more grown-up, you know?'

Lucy nodded and picked out a black T-shirt. 'Here, try this. Black is good for "sophisticated", especially if you wear it with the right accessories.'

I took off the blue top I was wearing and was just pulling the black T-shirt over my head when the door opened.

'Oh hi, Lucy,' said Mum, popping her head round the door. 'I didn't know you were here. Er, Izzie, I'm just popping out to the garden cen . . . What the . . . ?'

I'd tried to get the T-shirt over my head and down before she noticed, but it was too late. Old eagle eyes had seen it.

'Izzie! Is that a *stud* through your belly button?'

Lucy looked like she wanted to crawl under the bed.

'No.' I pulled my T-shirt down as far as it would go.

She entered the room. 'Let me see.'

'Oh please, Mum, leave it.'

'Let. Me. See. It,' she demanded.

Reluctantly, I lifted my T-shirt and her face turned to stone.

'When did you have that done?'

'Yesterday.'

'Where?'

'Camden.'

'Did you know about this, Lucy?' asked Mum, turning to Lucy who was staring at the floor. Lucy looked up at me anxiously and I managed to quickly shake my head behind Mum's back. I didn't want her getting in trouble with my mum for something I'd decided to do. Lucy shook her head.

Mum turned back to me. She looked furious. 'Take it out, this instant.'

'I can't,' I said.

'You can and you *will.*'

'No, really. You're not supposed to take it out for weeks, otherwise the hole will heal over.'

'You take that stud out this instant, young lady. No one gave you permission to have it put in. We never even discussed it.'

'Only because I knew you'd say no.'

'Exactly,' said Mum. 'And I'm saying no now.'

'You should have knocked,' I said, suddenly feeling angry. If she'd knocked, I could have got the T-shirt on and none of this would be happening. 'You're always walking in when I'm doing private things. I want a lock on my door.'

'Er, got to go,' said Lucy, getting up and heading for the door. 'Um, er, catch you later, Iz.'

And with that, she fled.

Lucy's Top Tips for Making the Most of Yourself

- Stand up straight. Don't slouch or hunch over. Think supermodel and strut your stuff.
- Eat healthy food. Hair and skin glow on a good diet and are dull on a stodgy junk food diet.
- Have regular pampering sessions, even if they're DIY at home. You'll get the idea that you're worth it, then others will pick up on this.
- Pay attention to detail: nails, hands, feet, eyebrows, skin.
- Keep hair clean and well cut. It's Murphy's Law – the day you put off washing your hair is the day you'll bump into someone you fancy.
- Save up and buy one wonderful item that makes you feel fabulous whenever you put it on.
- Wear underwear that fits properly and looks good.
- Think positively. Of all the things you wear, your expression is the one that people see first. If you are miserable and feel bored with yourself, others will pick up on that.
- Invest in a fab pair of sunglasses for days when you feel tired and not at your best.
- Ninety percent of looking good comes from confidence. Believe in yourself. Everyone has it in them to look wonderful in their own individual way.
- Find out what suits you as an individual. A designer label doesn't guarantee it will look fab on you.

Chapter 4

Loud Lady

Of course Mum got her way. I begged, I pleaded, I offered to do the washing up for the next month, but there's no arguing with her when she's got a strop on and this one was major. After a long lecture about infections, looking cheap, going behind her back, blah de blah de blah, she made me take out the stud. She even waited outside the bathroom door while I did it, then demanded that I hand it to her.

'I'll put this in the bin,' she said, wrapping it in a tissue like it was dog's doo-doo. 'And don't think we've finished, Isobel. You and I are going to sit down later and have words.' And with that, she headed down the stairs and out, slamming the front door behind her.

Words, I thought. Huh. Well, it's going to be her saying

them all because I'm never going to speak to her again. Ever.

As soon as I heard the car engine start up I rang Lucy, but her mobile was off. I dialled Nesta's number.

'Oh, you poor thing,' she sympathised, after I'd filled her in on the latest. 'After all you went through as well.'

'I know. She's gone to the garden centre in a huff. Poor plants, that's all I can say. You know they say that they're sensitive to vibes – well, I bet they all wilt when she walks in.'

'What does Angus say about the stud?'

Angus is my stepdad. I nicknamed him The Lodger when he and Mum first got together, as it was the only way I could deal with him and his daughters, Amelia and Claudia. But we get on OK now, so I call him by his proper name. He tends to stay out of it when Mum and I aren't getting on.

'Dunno. Nothing. He's hiding in the greenhouse, feeding geraniums or something equally boring. Is this what Sundays are about when you get old? Plants? I hope it never happens to me, Nesta. Anyway, Mum's being totally unreasonable. Lucy's parents are totally cool about her stud. It's not fair. I mean, it's not like I've got pregnant or become a drug addict or anything. I mean, what is her problem?'

'Maybe you should have told her you *were* pregnant,' said Nesta. 'You know, gone in with a long face and said, Mum I have something to tell you, then come out with this long list of *really* awful things. All fictitious, of course. Then, when she was totally freaked, you'd say, No, it's not true. But, oh . . . one tiny thing: I *have* had my belly button pierced. By then, she'd have been so relieved, she'd probably even have offered to pay for it.'

'D'er, why didn't I think of that?' I laughed. 'Look, do you fancy meeting me in Muswell Hill? I've had an idea.'

'What?'

'Tell you when I see you,' I said. 'Meet me in Ruby in the Dust in half an hour.'

'Izzie . . . what are you up to?'

'Tell you later.'

I raced up to Muswell Hill and, luckily, the shop I wanted was open, even though it was Sunday. I went in and headed for the back, where I knew they kept their jewellery displays. The quicker I get a new stud in, the better, I thought.

I found a perfect one. It was really pretty, silver with a square glass stone that reflects all the colours of the rainbow.

I made my purchase then went to Ruby in the Dust café where I headed straight for the ladies. Once inside, I locked the door and unwrapped my new stud. I know Del said you had to wait a few weeks, but I have no choice, I thought as I pulled up my T-shirt. Oh god, I don't think I can do this, I said to myself, as I looked at the tiny hole. It was scabbing over already and the area around it looked red and raw. I poked at the skin. It felt bruised and sore. No pain, no gain, I thought, and I took a deep breath and pushed the stud through in one quick go. 'Ow, ow, *OWWW* . . .'

There was a knock on the door. 'Are you all right in there?' called a woman with a very loud voice.

'Yes, fine,' I said, sitting on the loo for a moment to catch my breath and dab my eyes, which had started watering as the stud went through.

'You going to be long?' the voice boomed again.

'Just a minute.' I stood up and quickly wiped my belly button area with some water from the tap, then opened the door.

The lady outside gave me a strange look as I came out, so I gave her what I hoped was a reassuring smile, headed back into the café and made for the window seat.

I ordered a large hot chocolate and leaned back, trying to relax. After a while, I began to wonder if I'd done the wrong thing by buying the new stud. I hadn't really thought about it too much in the heat of the moment – only that Mum wasn't going to stop me. I'm not a baby any more, although she treats me like one sometimes. But maybe I'd gone a bit far by defying her this much. And I also wondered if it was worth it, as my belly button was stinging like anything.

I began to wish Mum was more like Dad. He's really cool. They split up yonks ago and he's remarried now, with a little boy. I don't think Dad would have objected to me getting my belly button pierced for a minute. He married one of his mature students and she has *three* earrings in her right ear. She's pretty cool too.

Just at that moment, I noticed a boy come in and sit on a sofa to my right. He looks familiar, I thought, then a rush of heat flooded through me. It was the guy from the park yesterday, only today he was dressed in jeans and a denim jacket instead of his black leathers. He didn't appear to notice me and as he sat waiting to be served, he started either playing a game or text messaging on his mobile.

A few seconds later, the woman from the loos came out and sat at the table behind him. The moment she sat down, her mobile rang. I couldn't help but turn to look at her when she answered. She talked *so* loud. You would have thought the person at the other end was deaf. Maybe she's talking to an ageing parent or someone, I thought. But then she finished that call and started another. She *still* talked really loud. The whole café could hear what she was saying and she seemed completely oblivious. The guy from the park turned around, glanced at her, then over at me. He raised his eyebrows as if to say, 'Some people.'

For the next ten minutes, the café customers got to know her life story intimately – she was having chicken for dinner, but cooking fish for Duchess, her cat. She was seeing John, whoever he was, at the weekend and he had a nasty rash on his ankle, so she thought he should see a doctor. And on and on and *on* at top volume. A few people gave her disapproving looks, but she didn't register them. On one call, she asked whoever she was talking to to ring her back and gave her number. I glanced over at Park Boy and I could swear that he was writing it down. What's he up to? I wondered. He can't possibly fancy her, she must be at least forty. Then at last, at *last,* Loud Lady got up to leave and the café was peaceful again. You could almost hear everyone breathe a sigh of relief.

From where I was sitting, I could see the woman exit the café, walk a few metres down the road and stand at a bus stop.

And then her mobile rang. As she answered it, I noticed that Park Boy was also on his phone.

'Is that 07485 95539?' he asked. That's definitely Loud Lady's number, I thought as I watched him, intrigued as to what he was up to.

I turned to look out the window at the bus stop where, sure enough, I saw Loud Lady nod her head.

'Well, this is the Mobile Phone Police,' said Park Boy. 'And it has come to our attention that you have the *loudest* voice ever recorded on our sound monitors. We're going to have to ask you to tone it down or else your phone will be confiscated.' Then he put his phone aside.

I burst out laughing and watched as Loud Lady looked

around her in bewilderment. Park boy caught my eye and laughed too. Excellent, I thought, and I hope he comes over. He seems like a real laugh. He didn't come over, though. He just went back to playing on his phone, so I went back my chocolate and gazed out the window, trying to look cool. After a few minutes, I decided I probably looked more vacant than cool, so I decided to write a song about him.

Nesta arrived about ten minutes later, full of apologies for being late. I glanced over at Park Boy, but he still had his head down, focused on his phone. Weird, I thought. Boys *always* look up when Nesta makes an entrance. They can't help it. She's half Italian, half Jamaican and that adds up to Stunning with a capital S. With her long silky black hair and dark exotic looks, she's a boy magnet.

As Nesta settled herself down, the boy *finally* got up. Oh, here we go, I thought, I knew it. He won't come over to me, but now he's seen Nesta, suddenly he's interested.

But no, he went straight out of the door. As he walked past the window, he glanced at me and winked. I smiled back. He didn't even glance at Nesta.

Dark Rider

Whenever I see him, I know it's right to be wrong.
I live and breathe him, but I've got to be strong.
Nobody likes him 'cause he thinks it's cool to be bad,
But deep down inside him, I'm sure there's good
to be had.
I should turn away when he's riding down the street,
But a blur of steel and black leather makes my heart
skip a beat.

Dark rider, fly my way and thrill me with your thunder.
Steely strider, I'm just looking for a smile.
Kick it over and accelerate, take me with you
miles and miles.
Right or wrong, what's going on, I've got to move on.

Chapter 5

Peculiar
Parents

Mum was in the kitchen chopping peppers when I got back from Muswell Hill. I took a deep breath and prepared myself for the inevitable. Just bite the bullet, I told myself. Let her have her say, look apologetic, then escape to the safety of my room.

'Izzie . . .' Mum began.

Izzie? I thought. What's going on? She calls me Isobel when she's mad. Was everything OK, then? I was still determined not to speak to her, though, only the requisite, yes, no, sorry, sorry. But as she went on, I began to feel *really* rotten. In her own way, I could see that she was trying to be understanding. I don't get her at all sometimes. I'd mentally prepared myself for the 'words', but she was being really nice, a total turnaround since this morning.

Maybe this is some new kind of torture, I thought, as she looked at me with concern. Or maybe she's been reading one of those 'How to deal with your mad teenage daughter' books. That's probably it. I don't know. Whatever it was, my new mellow mum kind of threw me. She was all, Are you all right? Did you get some lunch? Is there anything you want to talk about? You know I have your best interests at heart, and so on. I felt *awful*. I'd much rather be bawled out, I thought, because now I feel guilty as hell that I've got a new stud in. Hell's bells and poo. Sometimes I just can't win.

After the 'words', she offered to drive me over to Dad's, as I'd arranged to have supper there.

'Er, no thanks, Mum,' I said. 'I promised I'd drop in at Ben's on the way, just for half an hour to run through some of the songs for the gig next Saturday.'

She rolled her eyes. 'You're never in these days, Izzie. Look, call me from your dad's later, I'll come and get you.'

'Oh, don't worry, Mum,' I said. 'I'll get Dad to drop me.'

'Well, don't be too late,' she called after me as I headed for the door.

The boys were already there when I got to Ben's house in Highgate. There are four of them in the band: Ben, who's the lead vocalist and plays guitar and keyboard, Mark on bass, Elliot, also on keyboard, and Biff on drums. The band's called King Noz and they've made quite a name for themselves locally, playing gigs in pubs and local schools. I'm not officially in the band, but when I started going out with Ben, I sang a few numbers with them and now I've become a regular.

The boys were all out in the garage, going over some of the songs for Saturday. I say garage, but it's really a den/music studio. Ben's dad works as a sound engineer at the BBC and he converted the garage into a studio for Ben to rehearse in. It's totally brilliant in there. At the beginning of summer, Ben and I went down to the East End and bought loads of silk suit lining fabric, which we draped all over the garage, from the ceiling and walls. He put up posters of Krishna, Buddha and Guru Nanak and we persuaded his dad to collect this old sofa and chair that we'd spotted on a skip a few streets away. It's a really funky room now – it looks like an Arabian tent and it smells eastern as well, because he burns the joss sticks I got him for his birthday – lavender and amber ones. They smell fab. Ben gave me a key to the room when we were going out and he hasn't asked for it back, which is good of him. He said I could go there if ever I want to hang out on my own and get away from home. His parents are really cool and never go in. They're not daft, because I think if the band rehearsed in the house, they'd have gone mad with all the din.

Ben adjusted his glasses and looked up from one of the song sheets. 'So, Iz, got any new material?'

'Almost,' I said. 'I'm cooking a few ideas.'

Ben nodded. 'Well, let me have a look when you've got something down.'

'Will do,' I said and I kicked my shoes off and lay on the sofa. The boys started jamming, so I closed my eyes and drifted off. I've no regrets about finishing with Ben, I thought. Everyone said I was mad, as we got on so well, but the excitement had gone. We'd become mates, that's all. I wanted something more. Though I think I'll probably stay friends with Ben for life. He's the type of person that's really easy to be with – laid back, like nothing ever phases him. Not even me finishing with him. He was like, Whatever you want, babe.

My thoughts turned to the boy in the café this morning and I felt a shiver of anticipation. I wondered who he was, what he was into and if I'd bump into him again. It was weird seeing him twice in just two days. I'm a great believer in fate and I think that if something's meant to happen it will. I looked at my watch. It was only six. Dad lives in a flat near Chalk Farm, behind the shops on Primrose Hill Road. Maybe I'll get the tube to Camden then walk through the park over to Dad's instead of going up the main road, I thought. See if Park Boy's around.

At that moment, a noise to my right distracted me. I opened my eyes to see Biff over at the tap at the back wall. The others couldn't see what he was doing, but I could. He was filling a plastic bag with water. Biff's a bit of a nutter and likes nothing better than a water fight. I decided to get out while I was still dry. Last week, I'd joined in with gusto, hurling water bombs like the best of them, but . . . I don't know. Suddenly, it all seemed a bit childish. I wasn't in the mood. I felt restless, so I decided to go off to the park to see if fate had anything more interesting to offer.

On the journey down, my sense of anticipation grew. I really hoped Park Boy would be there. It was a lovely summer's evening and it felt like there was magic in the air. As I walked from Camden to Primrose Hill, there were loads of people around, standing outside the pubs, sitting outside cafés. For some reason, it felt really romantic. I walked up Parkway then right and along and into the park. As I walked through, there was no sign of him and I couldn't help feeling disappointed. Never mind, I told myself, what will be, will be. Anyway, he might have a girlfriend. All the fanciable boys are usually involved, one way or another.

As I got closer to Dad's flat, my thoughts turned to another cute boy. Tom. He's my three-year-old half-brother. One of my favourite things is giving him his nighttime bath, but he was already in bed when I got there.

Dad and Anna were just ordering an Indian takeaway and they ordered a mixed vegetable one for me, as I've been vegetarian for the last year. When the food arrived, we settled down to a really nice supper. It's always so relaxed at Dad's. The total opposite of Mum's, where there's not a thing out of place and everything is pristine and clean. Here, there are books, magazines and mess everywhere. It looks lived-in, not like the Ideal Home display at Mum's.

'Got a new book for you, Izzie,' said Dad, throwing me a paperback. '*The Catcher in the Rye,* by JD Salinger. I think you'll enjoy it.'

'Thanks,' I said. He's always giving me stuff to read. He lectures in English literature and sometimes I think that he forgets that I'm his daughter and imagines I'm one of his students. Some of the books he gives me are OK, but some of them are heavy going. I try and read them all, though, as I don't want him to think that I don't appreciate it.

Inevitably, Dad asked how things were at home, so I told him about the stud incident. I thought that if I could get him on my side, maybe Mum would come around to the idea. I *do* have two parents after all, and even though I live with Mum, she shouldn't have the final say about *everything*.

'So, would you have objected?' I asked.

Dad smiled. 'Don't grow up *too* soon, will you, Izzie?'

'No, course not. Anyway, how can you grow up *too* soon? You're meant to grow up and go through changes, aren't you? And I'm going into Year Ten next week, so that's moving on. And *don't* change the subject . . .' Dad always does this when I try and get him involved with anything that's happening at home. He kind of sidesteps it. 'Belly button stud. Would you have objected?'

'Probably not,' he said finally. 'Not if you really wanted one. It's your decision if you want to mutilate your body.'

So I told him I'd put a new stud in after Mum had confiscated the first one.

First he laughed, then he shook his head. 'Oh dear. Our Izzie's turning into a rebel. Your mother won't be happy about that, will she?'

'Well, she's not going to find out. And you won't tell her, will you?'

'No, of course not,' he said. 'But won't she find out? I mean, you *do* live in the same house.'

'That's the other thing,' I said. 'Would you have a word with her about letting me have a lock put on my bedroom door? She keeps walking in on me. I have no privacy at all.'

Dad looked at Anna and grimaced.

'Keep me out of it,' she said and started clearing away our takeaway dishes. Anna isn't a timid sort of person at all. She's very forthcoming with her opinions about most things, but I've noticed that she never says anything about my mum. Like Angus. He never says anything about Dad.

Dad looked at his hands. 'I don't know, Izzie. I don't

know if I'm the best one to go laying down the law about how things should be at home. She wouldn't like it.'

Poo, I thought. Everyone's scared of my mother. Even my dad. No wonder they split up.

After we'd cleared the kitchen, Anna asked if I wanted to stay and watch a film with them. I looked at my watch. It was half past eight. I'd told Mum I wouldn't be late, so if I left now, I could still stay in her good books.

'Are you sure I can't drop you?' asked Dad as I put on my jacket to go.

I shook my head. 'No, you stay and relax. I'll walk up to Camden and get the tube. It's still light and I've got my mobile.'

Finally he let me go and I set off for the tube. Once again, I chose the scenic route, past the shops at Primrose Hill, through the park, then along Regent's Park Road up to Parkway. Part of me was thinking that if fate had brought me and Park Boy together twice in two days, then it would bring us together again. But another part was thinking that there's no harm in giving fate a hand. That part was definitely winning the argument.

The light was beginning to fade when I reached the park gates, and normally I wouldn't walk through on my own, because I know that there are some dodgy people around and not to take stupid risks. But something inside of me was pushing me to go on. I'll be fine, I told myself, and I have my trusty mobile.

I glanced up the hill to my right as I set off along the path at the bottom of the park. There were a couple of girls sitting near the railings and I was pretty sure they were the ones that Park Boy was with the day before, but no sign of him. Apart from the girls, there weren't many other people about – only an old lady walking her dog and a man jogging.

As I got halfway down the path, I began to wonder if I'd made a mistake taking this route. It was very quiet and even though it wasn't dark yet, it didn't feel as safe as when there were loads of people about. I tried to remember TJ's tips for being out on your own at night. She's been working on a piece for the school mag about being street smart. Not walking in empty places at night, I thought, that was one of them.

I stepped up my pace, then glanced over my shoulder. Someone was on the path behind me. A boy in black. He put his head down when I turned. Was it Park Boy? I glanced again, but he'd left the path and was heading for the trees, so I couldn't see his face. He looked about same height as Park Boy, but I couldn't be sure that it was him. I could feel my heart beginning to pound as I glanced behind again. No sign of anyone. I don't like this, I thought. I looked across at the trees and could see movement, like someone was darting from tree to tree, trying to stay out of sight. My heart began to beat really fast and I felt my chest tighten with fear. Was it Park Boy playing some daft game? Then it dawned on me that even if it was, I didn't know him at all. Maybe he was some kind of weirdo.

I stopped for a moment to try and locate exactly where the person was. But whoever it was in the trees also stopped. I set off again, walking fast, but not quite breaking into a run yet. What shall I do? I thought. I could feel myself begin to panic and I got my mobile out of my pocket and put my thumb on the keypad, ready to phone Dad if I got into any trouble. He lived nearest and could be there in five minutes if I needed help. I took a *really* quick glance over my shoulder and saw the shape of someone on the path. Yeah, it is Park Boy, I decided, breathing a sigh of relief. Same denim jacket. Right, I thought. Let's see how *he* likes it when people disappear behind trees! As I turned a corner on the path, I snuck behind a tree and waited. I could hear the sound of footsteps approaching and as the Boy walked by, I leaped out.

'Park Police,' I yelled. 'What do you think you're playing at?'

A young lad with dark hair almost leaped out of his skin. He took one look at me and began to run as fast as he could away from me towards the gate. Whoever he was, he wasn't the one who had been following me. As I watched him scarper, I heard someone laughing behind me. I swung around and Park Boy stepped out with a huge grin on his face.

'You *creep!*' I yelled. 'You really scared me.'

'Er, excuse me,' he said and pointed at the young lad in the distance, who was still running. 'I think it's *you* who's scaring people. Park Police!'

'I thought he was you. What were *you* doing? You were following me, hiding in the trees.'

'I thought you *saw* it was me,' he said, pointing back up the path. 'Way back there.'

'Yeah, but I don't know you.'

'From the café, this morning . . .'

'I know. But I don't *know* you . . .'

'Oh, right,' said the boy, then smiled. 'Josh Harper.' He pointed at the girls I'd passed. 'I'm with some mates. Do you want to come and join us?'

I looked behind me to the other side of the park, then towards the gate off to my left. I did a quick calculation. If I walked back over and hung out with them for a while, it would be late and I didn't fancy walking the path again when it was really dark, and I didn't want to act like I was a weed, asking one of them to come with me.

'Er, no thanks,' I said.

'Got to be home by curfew time?'

'*No.* Just . . .'

'Then chill,' he said and sat on the grass, smiling a really wicked smile. 'I won't bite you . . . least not until I've got to know you better.' He pulled out a can of lager from his jacket. 'Want a drink?'

I pulled a face. 'No thanks. Lager tastes disgusting.'

He laughed and reached into his other pocket and pulled out a small bottle of vodka. 'Prefer this?'

I shook my head again. 'What are you? A walking bar?'

'No, that's the lot.' He lifted his arms and leaned back on the grass, inviting me to go into his pockets. 'But you're welcome to go through my things, officer.'

I felt myself blushing and was glad that it was beginning to get dark. Hopefully he wouldn't notice.

'No, I believe you,' I said.

'So what's your name?'

'Izzie.'

'So, no vodka, no lager. What does Izzie like to drink?'

Actually Ribena Lite is my favourite at the moment but I didn't think it sounded very sophisticated. 'Er . . .'

Luckily I was saved from answering as my mobile rang. 'S'cuse me a sec.' I walked a few paces away to take the call. It was Mum. She sounded harassed.

'Where are you?'

'On my way home.'

'Why isn't your dad bringing you? I just called there and he said you were making your own way back.'

'I'll be back before it's dark.'

'Where exactly are you?'

'Just going into Camden tube station,' I fibbed.

'I'll pick you up at East Finchley, then.'

I switched off the phone and went back to Josh. He

looked highly amused. 'Mum and Dad wondering where their little girl is?'

'*No*. But I got to go. Er . . . things to do.'

'Sure.' He shrugged and got up to go back to his friends. 'See you around, kid.'

Kid, I thought as I walked away. What a cheek. Then I turned to sneak another look at him. He turned back at exactly the same time and laughed when he saw me glancing round. Ha, I thought as I set off for the tube. Caught you looking!

TJ's Tips for Being Streetwise

- Always keep a taxi number handy for times of emergency or times you can't reach someone you know. If you have a mobile, save the number in your address book.
- Keep your keys in your pocket in case someone ever steals your bag – that way at least you can get in your front door.
- It's a good idea to have a bag that you can wear diagonally over your body, so it's harder for someone to grab it and run.
- Don't walk in dark, secluded places. Use routes home that are well lit and where there are still people about, even if it means walking further.
- Don't make eye contact with strangers.
- If you ever feel you're being followed, get to a populated area as fast as possible and keep your mobile within reach but out of sight.
- Never hesitate to call and ask someone to pick you up if you've been stranded.
- If a stranger ever asks if you want a lift, always say no and that your dad is on his way and will be there any second. Then immediately phone the person you know who lives nearest.
- If ever travelling on the tube or train, always travel in a compartment with people in it. If they get off at a stop, leaving the carriage empty, get off with them and get into a carriage with people in it.
- If ever you are mugged, don't fight. Hand over your phone, watch or purse, then leg it.
- Walk confidently – head up and briskly.

Chapter 6

Zombie

'I've got a quiz to try out on you,' said Lucy, flopping on the sofa. 'It's just your kind of thing, Izzie – sort of a psychological test.'

We were all over at Nesta's the following evening. We spent the first twenty minutes swopping news and I'd filled them in on bumping into Josh again and the ongoing war with Mum. She was back to her usual mad self when she picked me up from the tube station the night before. Apparently when she phoned Dad to ask why I wasn't home yet, he mentioned that he knew about the belly button stud. She wasn't happy. Oh no. She spent the whole journey home going on about how he's too laid back when it comes to disciplining me, he's not the one who has to lay down the rules, the one who worries when I'm out late, wonders where I am and what I'm getting up to. I tried telling her that I could handle myself, but she wasn't really listening. No wonder Dad doesn't want to get involved. She gets so worked up over nothing.

It was good to get out of the house and over to Nesta's to see the girls and have some normal company.

'OK,' I said, sitting on the floor next to the sofa. 'Shoot.'

'You have to think of your three favourite animals,' said Lucy. 'Then remember them in order. Tell me when you've got them.'

We all sat and thought for a few minutes.

'OK, ready,' I said.

'And me,' chorused Nesta and TJ.

'OK,' said Lucy. 'Say them out loud and why you picked them. Nesta?'

'Cats because they're elegant and independent. Leopards because they're beautiful, and peacocks because they're stunning when they put their tails up and strut their stuff.'

Lucy laughed.

'What?' asked Nesta. 'What's so funny?'

'You'll find out in a minute,' said Lucy. 'OK, Iz?'

'Um, dolphins because they're friendly and intelligent, orang-utans because when you look into their eyes, you can tell they have these really wise old souls, and owls because they're meant to be wise, but if you ever take a good look at them, they're actually hysterically funny –

they can turn their heads round almost three hundred and sixty degrees.'

Lucy burst out laughing again.

'*What?*' I asked.

'You'll see in a minute. TJ?'

'Penguins because they're entertaining and have a funny walk, dogs because they're intelligent, loyal and playful, and meercats because they look after each other – they're really social animals.

'OK.' Lucy said, grinning. 'I'll tell you what it all means now. Your first choice was how you see yourself . . .'

'That's amazing,' I said. 'TJ picked penguins because they're entertaining, and you are, TJ. Dunno about the funny walk, though. And Nesta picked cats because they're elegant and independent. It's really true.'

'And you said dolphins because they're friendly and intelligent,' said Nesta. 'That's true as well.'

'OK, what do the other choices mean?' asked Nesta.

'Second one is how others see you and the last one is how you really are.'

'We see you as an orang-utan . . .' laughed Nesta, pointing at me.

'Yeah, fat and hairy,' I said.

Nesta laughed again. 'We're going to have to work on your self-esteem, girl.'

'But it's more the reason *why* you picked them that's revealing, not the animal so much,' said Lucy. 'And Izzie said because when she looks at an orang-utan, she sees a wise old soul. That's *exactly* how I see you, Iz.'

'And you really are a peacock,' said TJ, pointing at Nesta.

Nesta's face clouded. 'Proud as a peacock. Oh dear.'

'No,' said Lucy. 'You didn't say that. You said you liked peacocks because they're stunning when they strut their stuff. Nothing could be more true in your case.'

'And others do see you as beautiful,' said TJ. 'You said leopards for your second one because they're beautiful. Second one's how others see you, right, Lucy?'

Lucy nodded.

Nesta started strutting around the room. 'Yeah. And you're an owl, Izzie. Why did you say you liked them?'

'Because they can turn their heads three hundred and sixty degrees.' I tried to do it, but nope, wouldn't go.

TJ pulled a face. 'And I'm a meercat.'

'But all the ones you chose, you said were because they're playful, intelligent and loyal,' said Lucy. 'That's exactly how you are, TJ. Don't you see – your choices reveal a lot about your character.'

'Kind of like how what you wear reveals who you are as well,' I said. 'So what did you pick, Luce?'

'Horse, ostrich, dog. Horses because they're gentle, ostriches because they're funny and dogs because they're faithful and fun.'

'Spot on,' said TJ.

'OK,' said Nesta. 'I'm going to strut my stuff into the kitchen. Who wants what?'

'Diet Coke,' said TJ.

'Same,' said Lucy.

'Izzie?' asked Nesta.

'How long are your parents out for?' I asked.

'Until about ten-thirty, I think,' said Nesta. 'They've gone to see a movie. Why?'

I eyed the drinks cabinet under the bookshelf behind the sofa. They had an amazing collection of spirits and liqueur – some I'd never heard of. Nesta saw me looking and went and stood next to them. 'What can I get you, Madam? Gin and tonic? Vodka and orange? Eggflip and marmite?'

I went and stood next to her and put my finger under my chin. 'Hmm, I'm not sure, barman. What do you recommend?'

'Chocolate milkshakes with marshmallows,' said Nesta, heading for the door. 'How does that sound?'

'Shall we try a *drink* drink?' I asked. 'You know, while your parents are out. Just a taste to see what we might like.'

'I've tried most of them,' said Nesta, 'and I can tell you, they're pretty yuck. Whisky is sour, vodka is tasteless and gin tastes like lighter fluid.'

'Since when have you been drinking lighter fluid?' I asked.

Nesta screwed her face up. 'You know what I mean. Not very nice.'

'I'd like to try one,' I said. 'See, like what Lucy was saying about people's choices revealing who they are – I don't know what I like to drink.'

'But most of them taste awful, honest . . .' said Nesta.

'I know,' I said. 'I've tried some of Mum's when she's been out too. But you can mix them with other stuff, you know, to take away the taste of alcohol.'

'So, what's the point?' asked TJ.

'Well, you can't drink Sprite or Ribena Lite forever. It's looks a bit babyish sometimes.'

'Says who?' said TJ. 'I don't care. It's what tastes good to *me* that counts. I'm the one drinking it.'

'Yeah, but if you're with a load of older boys or something, or at a party, it might be good to ask for something more sophisticated.'

I glanced at the bookshelves and spotted a book tucked in with some recipe books. I pulled it out and read the title. '*Cocktails for City Nights*. How about we try one of these?' I flicked through the opening pages. 'There are loads here. Barracuda Bite, Moscow Mule . . . Oh, here's one for me. It's called Dirty Mother. What do you think? See what they taste like?'

Lucy came and read the list over my shoulder. 'Hey, TJ. How do you fancy trying a Screaming Orgasm?'

'Ex*scooth* me?' she giggled.

'It's made from Irish cream, Kahlua, vodka and amaretto.' I looked at the bottles. 'Yeah, your mum has all of those.'

Nesta came back over to the drinks cabinet and looked at the bottles. 'Shall we?' she asked with a mischievous look on her face.

'Count me out,' said TJ from where she was lying on the floor. 'I don't like alcohol. I tried some red wine once and it tasted like ink.'

'Yeah, but some of these sound really nice,' I said, still reading. 'They have juice and liqueurs and some even have cream in them. I'll make you a special one. A TJ Watts.'

'The milkshake sounded good to me,' said TJ. 'That's what I fancy. Did you know that one glass of spirits has something like three hundred calories in it? I'd rather use my quota up on chocolate.'

'Oh, come on,' I said. 'Where's your spirit of adventure? Let's make a few of them. Just for a taste.'

Lucy looked worried and glanced at Nesta. 'But won't your parents notice?' she asked. 'I mean, if the levels in the bottles have gone down, they'll know it was us.'

'We're not going to drink *that* much, Lucy,' I said. 'Just experiment a bit. Last night when Josh asked what I wanted to drink, I felt stupid. In future, I want to be able to answer with confidence. I think that's part of being a grown-up, knowing what you like. But I haven't got a clue. I think it's part of finding out who you are – you know, whether you like coffee or tea, spirits or wine and so on.'

TJ grinned. 'Well if you're an orang-utan, we'd better get you some banana juice.'

'Yeah right. Very refined. *Not,*' I said.

Lucy started laughing. 'Drink? Oh, thank you, darling,' she said in a posh voice. 'I'll have . . .' She glanced at the cocktail book. 'Yes, I'll have a Tidal Wave – no, maybe not, sounds pretty lethal. No, make mine . . .' This time she made her voice go squeaky. '. . . a Coconut Highball.'

Nesta read over her shoulder and made her face go stupid. 'And I'll have a Zombie.'

'That sounds nice,' I said. 'It's rum, pineapple, lemon and orange.'

'OK,' said Nesta. 'Here's the deal. We mix up a few and have a little taste of each other's. OK?'

'And if the levels are down a bit,' said Lucy, 'we can fill the bottles up with a bit of water. That's what my brother Lal did when he tried Dad's whisky the other week. Dad never noticed.'

We spent a short time picking the ones we liked the sound of, then checking to see if Nesta's parents had the ingredients.

'They've got most of them,' said Nesta. 'People always give them weird liqueurs at Christmas and they never get touched unless Mum is making some exotic dessert.'

I picked a White Russian as I thought that sounded really cool. Nesta ended up choosing one called a Kamikaze, TJ went for a Piña Colada and Lucy decided that she had to try the Screaming Orgasm.

'Just in case I never get off with a boy ever again and never actually get to have sex,' she said, laughing. 'At least I can say truthfully that I've had a screaming orgasm.'

'Yeah. Who needs boys?' I asked, running my finger down the index. 'There's one here called Sex With a Shark.'

'Think I'll pass on that,' said Lucy. 'I'm trying to give up sharks. Rats are more my thing. Love rats.'

Nesta went and got juices and cream from the fridge and we spent the next ten minutes pouring and stirring. Once our drinks were ready, we took a sip of the one we made, then a sip of each other's. My White Russian tasted fantastic, so after the others had a sip, I drank all of it. It had a load of cream and coffee liqueur in it and tasted really sweet. Fab. Nesta didn't like hers. 'Too sour,' she said and handed it to me. I took a sip. Yuck. She was right. 'Too much lime,' I said.

'Stick to the sweet ones,' I said. 'Here, I'll make you one. A Nesta special.' I poured some blackcurrant liqueur, a shot of gin and some vodka into a glass and swirled it around. It's simple, I thought. You just mix up what you like until it tastes good. Nesta didn't like that either, though. Waste not, want not, I thought, adding a bit of lemonade. Tastes like Ribena. So I slugged it back.

TJ only took a sip of hers. 'I thought we were just

trying them,' she said. 'Not drinking the whole thing. We might get drunk.'

'Cowardy custard,' I said. I took a taste of Lucy's. Mmmm, I thought. Also quite nice. It tasted really sweet and almondy.

'It's got amaretto in it,' she said. 'Mum puts it in her cake mix at Christmas.'

'Let's try another,' I said, raising my glass.

Nesta pulled a face. 'Not for me, thanks. I learned my lesson at your first gig with King Noz, remember?'

'All forgotten,' I said happily. It was around last Christmas and some plonker had given her a pile of champagne. It was my first performance with King Noz and I was really nervous about it, then Nesta got tiddly and hogged the limelight by dancing madly in front of everyone when they were supposed to be listening to the band. I suppose it was funny, looking back, but at the time, I was really miffed that she'd stolen all the attention.'

'I felt quite ill afterwards, if I remember rightly,' said Nesta.

'Can't take your drink,' I teased her. 'OK. Lucy, do you want to try another one?'

Lucy wrinkled her nose. 'Haven't finished this one yet. You're not supposed to slug them back, you know, especially if you want to be more grown-up. You're supposed to sip, like a lady. Like this . . .' She took a mouthful and started gargling it and making her eyes go cross-eyed at the same time.

TJ, Nesta and I all creased up and took mouthfuls of ours, then gargled as well.

'Really, though, Izzie,' said Nesta when we'd stopped laughing. 'I don't think you're supposed to knock them back. And you've had two plus some of ours already.'

'I'm fine,' I said. 'Just one more.' I felt like being reckless and daring for a change. Everyone always thinks I'm the sensible one, I thought. Oh, sensible Izzie, she has all the answers. But I don't, not really. I'm just a mad old orang-utan. I looked back at the index and picked another cocktail. 'I'm going to try one of these Tequila Sunrises. I think that sounds really nice, don't you? And it's mainly orange juice, so it will be OK, won't it?'

Nesta shrugged and started to put the tops back on the bottles. 'I guess, but don't blame me if you feel like crapola tomorrow.'

I think this will be my drink, I said to myself, as I poured some tequila and orange into a glass. My brain was starting to feel slightly fuzzy, but in a nice way, as I poured in a generous measure. Slightly bitter, I thought when I tasted it. Needs something else. I added a dash of whisky and tried that. Nope, still not nice. So I added a tiny bit of Martini. No, yuck, that one doesn't work at all. I put it to one side.

After that, the others sat down and began to watch

telly. I was feeling too good to just slob on the sofa, so I started reading through the cocktail book again.

'I'm going to become an expert,' I said. 'Cocktail queen. When I've got a flat of my own, I'll have *all* these drinks. A whole wall of them, like in a bar. And I'll have the fluorescent ones as well, the ones that make drinks blue or green. Like *really* sopisti . . . no, I mean, soristi . . . no, *sophisticated*. S'a hard word to say, that. Isn't it? Sopis . . . tic . . . ated. Never realised that before.'

'Izzie, you're drunk,' said TJ from the sofa.

'No, I'm not,' I said. I wasn't. At least I didn't think so. I felt perfectly fine. 'Don't be silly. But I do feel good.' Then I spotted some crème de menthe. 'There's a green one. I bet that tastes nice mixed with Bailey's. My gran always has that, at Christmas. It tastes like it has chocolate in it.' I poured a small amount of each into a glass.

Nesta got up, took the glass out of my hand and took a sip. She almost spat it out. 'It tastes of toothpaste mixed with liquified After Eight. *Yee-uck*. Way too sickly.'

I took the glass off her and swigged it down. 'Mmm. I like it. S'nice. Chocolatey.'

'Come and sit down,' said Lucy. 'We're going to start a film.'

'OK,' I said. 'Just going to the loo.' I started to walk towards the door and that's when I became aware that maybe the drinks were stronger than I'd thought. My legs seemed to have turned to jelly and the room began to sway. Oops, I thought, as I reached out to the wall for support. Am OK. Just a bit . . . wobbly. Walk straight.

Lucy, Nesta and TJ were half laughing and half looking at me with concern. 'S'OK,' I said. 'I'm fine.' I *was* fine. It was *them* who were out of focus.

I made my way out to the corridor and realised I was having a very hard time walking in a straight line. I made it to the bathroom and switched on the light. Very, very bright, I thought, as I sat on the loo and tried to pull myself together. Fine, I told myself, feeling fine. But my vision had gone all blurry and I was beginning to feel a tad nauseous.

There was a knock on the door, then Lucy's voice. 'Izzie. You still in there?'

'Yeah.'

'You've been in there for ages,' she said. 'You OK?'

I made myself get up, but the room seemed to be spinning. 'Yeah. Fine,' I said. I opened the door and giggled.

Lucy raised an eyebrow. 'Come and sit down.'

I followed her back to the sitting room, trying once again to walk in a straight line. Funny feeling this, I thought. Sort of giggly, but blurry at the same time. As we reached the sitting room door, I was vaguely aware of Nesta's brother, Tony coming into the house.

This would be a good time to stop and stand still, I decided. Prop myself up against the wall.

Tony looked at me quizzically. 'You all right?' he asked.

'Oops.' I laughed as I leaned back on the wall and knocked a picture frame squiff.

He gave me a funny look, then went into the sitting room. I followed, or rather fell, in after him. He took in the bottles and glasses. 'You girls have been having fun, I see,' he said.

'Izzie's drunk as a skunk,' said Nesta from the sofa.

'I am *not . . .*' I said. I wasn't. I really wasn't. Just felt a bit blurry and in need of a lie-down. On the carpet behind the sofa seemed like a good place, so I knelt down and crawled there. It felt nice and cool, so I curled up and closed my eyes. Euumm. Feel a bit funny, I thought, and opened one eye. All I could see was under the sofa and the skirting board. This is what mice see, I thought. Arrr. Sweet. A mouse's view on life. But fine. Fine. Best have a little sleep.

'Do you want to watch the movie?' asked Lucy, popping her head over the sofa top. 'We've got *Titanic.*'

I waved my hand at her. 'No, you jo astead. Just having a liddle sleep.'

After that I was vaguely aware of voices and the telly. They sounded very distant. 'She hasn't had tequila, has she?' I heard Tony say.

Nesta shrugged. 'Don't know. Think so.'

'Prepare for the hangover from hell, Iz, my old pal,' called Tony over the sofa.

'Okeee dokeee,' I said without opening my eyes.

'Tequila's lethal,' said Tony. I don't know who he was talking to, though. It was way too much effort to open my eyes. My eyelids seemed to have stuck together somehow. 'Even some of the most hardy drinkers can't take it. Very nasty side effects. What else has she had?'

'Blackcurrant liqueur, Bailey's . . .'

I must have drifted off because the next thing I knew there was a bitter smell of coffee. It made me want to retch. Tony was holding a cup next to my nose. 'Come on, Iz. Have a sip.'

I pulled a face and rolled away from him. 'Don't like coffee. I'm vegetarian. Want to sleep.'

Tony began to laugh. 'Did nobody ever tell you Lesson Number One in drinking, Izzie? Don't mix your drinks.'

'Won't,' I moaned. 'Fact, won't drink again. Been very, very stupid. Kay, go way now, need to sleep.'

There was the sound of the front door opening and footsteps in the hall.

'*Ohmigod,*' I heard Nesta cry. 'Quick, put the glasses under the sofa.'

The sitting room door opened and I heard the girls scrabbling about, then another voice. It sounded vaguely familiar. 'What in *heaven's* name is going on here?' said Nesta's mum.

'And why is Izzie lying behind the sofa?' asked her dad.

Oops, I thought, as I tried to roll into a ball and make myself invisible.

Lucy's Quiz

Name your three favourite animals, birds or fish in
order of preference. Say why you've chosen them.
First choice reveals: how you see yourself.
Second choice reveals: how others see you.
Third choice reveals: how you really are.
It's the adjectives chosen to say why the animal
has been picked that are revealing,
more than the animal itself.

Chapter 7

Orang–utans in the Mist

Ooooh. Strange dreams. Very strange dreams. Orang–utans in the mist. Snowy forests with penguins eating blackcurrants. Don't feel very well, I thought, when I woke up the next day and tried to open my eyes. It appears someone glued my eyelids together in the night. And my *head*. Oof. Somebody's doing a drum solo in there. I turned over and looked at the clock. Half past ten. Oops. I rolled on to my back and looked at the ceiling. How did I get home? I asked myself. I could vaguely remember Angus turning up. He must have driven me back. Don't remember seeing Mum. Oh God. Mum. I pulled the duvet over my head. Think I'll stay under here from now on. Probably best I never get up again. Ever.

Half an hour later, I was woken again by my mobile. I

cautiously got out of bed, grappled around for my bag and found the phone.

'How are you?' asked Lucy.

I rubbed my eyes. 'Bit fragile, to tell the truth.'

Lucy laughed. 'Serves you right. What did your mum say?'

'Haven't seen her yet. I guess she'll be at work now. Don't remember much.'

'You were hysterical,' said Lucy. 'Falling about all over the place when Angus arrived. At one point, he tried to pick you up and you told him to bog off.'

'Oh *no*, I didn't, did I?' I moaned. 'Well, that's it, isn't it? I will never ever *ever* drink again.'

'Right. What, not even water?'

'Oh haha, Lucy. I mean alcohol. Not if it makes you feel like this.'

'Oh yeah, that reminds me. Tony asked me to pass on his infallible hangover cure.'

'Good. What is it?'

'Don't drink the night before,' she laughed.

'Oh, very funny. Are the others in trouble?'

'Nesta is. My dad picked me and TJ up and we just ran out to the car and didn't tell him anything. But Nesta's been grounded today. She's really miffed because it was your idea to try the drinks.'

'Oh Go-*od*,' I groaned. 'I'll phone her and apologise. Got to go and lie down again now, Lucy. Sorry. Call you soon.'

'Drink a load of water,' said Lucy. 'That's what Mum does whenever she's had too much to drink.'

After I hung up, I saw that someone had put a glass of water by the bed. Mum probably. I dutifully drank it, then lay down for a while longer. I felt dreadful, like I'd been run over by a bus. After another hour, I finally made it downstairs to get some more water.

Angus works from home some days and this was one of them. He looked up from his desk as I passed his study on the way to the kitchen. I gave him a weak smile and prepared myself for the telling off.

'How are you feeling?' he asked.

'Rotten, if you must know.'

He chuckled. 'Enough to drive you to drink, isn't it?'

I went to stand in the doorway. 'Aren't you mad with me?'

He shook his head. 'But your mum is. She said to say that you're grounded and can't go over to Nesta's until school starts again.'

'It wasn't Nesta's fault. It was me who started it all. And I won't be doing it again in a hurry, I can tell you.'

Angus chuckled again. 'Never say never,' he said.

He's clearly never had a hangover like this, I thought, as I staggered into the kitchen.

Mum rang early in the afternoon and was true to her word. Grounded, she said. I couldn't go out until she said so, even though there wasn't much of the holidays left. I knew I didn't have a leg to stand on, literally on the night of the cocktails, so I didn't try and argue. I knew I'd blown it with her.

I decided to keep a diary of my imprisonment.

Day One:

First day of prison sentence. Don't mind staying in as feel pretty grotty. Began to feel marginally better after a ton of water.

Cleaned the house. Even though we have a cleaner, thought it was a good way to earn brownie points.

Belly button update. It's healing up nicely at last, phew. It's going to look great in a few weeks. Ha ha, Mum, you may have grounded me, but I've got a new belly button stud in. You can't control everything.

Worked on lyrics for new songs.

Thought about Josh. Thought a lot about Josh. He said 'See you around.' No chance of that, then — not for a while. Unless Mum relents and there's not much chance of that. Felt good when I saw him in the park last time. Sort of buzzy. Definitely different to being with Ben. They must be about the same age, but somehow Josh is more exciting. And he's taller.

Practised doing a new signature. If changing my image, then my handwriting is part of it. Covered about ten pages.

Practised snogging technique on the back on my hand. Think I may be going mad.

Tried on every stitch of clothing I own and managed to work out some pretty cool combinations. Black and black mainly, with some silver jewellery. Some of the tops I was going to throw out because I thought I'd grown out of them look good on second trying. Used to wear my clothes baggy, but now some of the T-shirts look just right – tight in the right places. Mum won't like it. She doesn't like anything. Mainly me.

TJ and Lucy came over and brought magazines. Amazingly, even though I was grounded, Angus let them in on the condition that I didn't tell Mum. He can be OK sometimes. Lucy did fantastic make-up on me to go with my new look. Dark eyes and sort of grape glossy lipstick. Definitely makes me look older and will look cool for the gig on Saturday – that is, if Mum lets me go. TJ asked me to do a piece for her mag on what to do when you're grounded. Don't think I'll include 'Practise snogging on the back of your hand', in case people at school think I'm a saddo. But I bet they all do it.

After they left, I practised my songs for the gig on Saturday. I'm only doing two this time, which is fine by me as I like sitting and listening as well as performing. Please, please God let Mum have mellowed by then.

Mum back at seven-thirty. Waited for le grando telling off, but it never came. She just looked disappointed, a look she's got down to perfection, if you ask me, but pretty upsetting all the same. Don't really like it when she's seriously mad with me.

Ate a tiny bit of supper. Tummy's still a bit funny. Cleared table, washed up – even the pans. Said sorry a million times. Smiled meekly at Mum and Angus. Am perfect daughter.

Called Nesta. Got her voicemail.

Listened to music. Worked on songs again.

Nothing on telly. Slept like a zombie (not the cocktail).

Day Two:

Called Nesta's mobile as don't want to risk her mum or dad picking up their home phone and giving me another telling-off. Got voicemail. She's obviously screening her calls and is still mad at me.

Feel restless. Surely two days in prison is enough? Called Mum at work to beg forgiveness, but she's in a meeting schmeeting. She'll probably only say that I can't go out until I've learned my lesson, so I don't really know why I'm bothering. Why doesn't she realise that I learnt my lesson on Day One? You don't have to tell me twice not to drink alcohol again. Never, never, never. I don't want to go through that again.

Colour coordinated my wardrobe. Only took five minutes as it's all black now.

Started reading The Catcher in the Rye. *Brilliant. At first, couldn't get into it as it's about this boy called Holden Caulfield who's been expelled from boarding school in America. Thought I couldn't relate. But as there was nothing else to do, I got into it and then I couldn't put it down. Even though it was written ages ago, in the nineteen forties, he's just like any normal teenager, and like me, questioning everything. Is it the same for teenagers the world over? Nothing seems to make sense any more and you don't know who you want to be, what you want to do, and in the meantime, you manage to upset* everyone.

Called Nesta. She picked up. Phew. Talked for half an hour. She said I should try calling Mum again as parents do tend to blow steam then calm down. Tried calling Mum again. She said she is prepared to let me go out as long as I let her know where I am and what I'm doing at all times. Felt very tempted to call her five minutes later from the bathroom to tell her I was on the loo, but resisted as that might be pushing my luck a bit.

So, goodbye diary. Prison sentence cut short. Time off for good behaviour. Mum said I can go out so I'm free! Ha ha, HEE HEE, cue maniacal laughter.

I put on my trainers and shorts and decided to go for a jog. It was drizzling, but felt really fresh, so I ran and ran and ran. After about twenty minutes, I heard a motorbike approaching. It screeched to a stop next to me.

'Izzie,' called Josh as I ran past him.

Murphy's Law, I said to myself as I stopped and turned. I *would* bump into him on the one day I have no make-up on, my hair's dripping with rain and I'm sweaty from running. Not my most alluring look, I thought as a raindrop fell off my nose. I decided to keep my head down and keep the conversation short.

'Um, hi,' I said.

He took off his helmet. 'Where have you been? I was hoping to see you in the park again. Didn't scare you off that night, did I? With the tree thing?'

'Um, no, course not,' I said to the pavement. 'Been busy.'

'What you doing tonight?'

'Not sure.' Actually I had told Ben I'd go round to go through my songs one last time before the gig, and I'd planned to go to Lucy's after that. But you *do* have to be flexible in life.

'A few of us are getting together later, if you want to meet up. Come and have a drink.'

I pulled a face.

'What?' he said.

'Drink.'

'What about drink?'

'Bad joojoo,' I answered, then decided I would tell him all about it without actually revealing that it was the first time I'd tried alcohol properly. 'Had a bit too much on Monday night. Never again.'

Josh laughed. 'Ah, hangover, eh? You know the best thing for that?'

'Don't drink the night before?'

He laughed and shook his head. 'Nah. Hair of the dog. Back on the horse, and so on.'

'No thanks,' I said. 'I've learned my lesson.'

'You sound like an old woman.'

'Last time you called me a kid,' I said. 'I can't win.'

He smiled. 'It's not a competition.'

'I wasn't . . .'

'Come on – we're meeting at Pond Square in Highgate. See you there, about five-thirty?'

'Maybe,' I said. 'I'll have to check with my social secretary.'

Josh laughed. 'Your mum and dad, you mean?'

'*No,*' I said. Actually I did mean my mum, but I wasn't going to tell him that. She'd already said that I could go to Ben's, so to do a quick detour to the square wouldn't be going much out of my way. I'd set off early. Mum would never know if I called her before I left, then again from Ben's. It would be worth it. Just for half an hour. 'OK. I'll be there.'

'Cool,' he said, and with that he roared off again.

Things to Do When You're Grounded

- Catch up on homework.
- Colour coordinate your wardrobe.
- Store shoes in boxes. Take a picture/Polaroid of each pair and stick it on the outside of the box for quick identification.
- Do some Feng Shui on your bedroom and get rid of all the clutter. If you haven't worn something for over a year, chuck it.
- Feng Shui your computer (tidy your desktop and clear up old files).
- Update your address book. Then update your diary.
- Start your bestselling novel. If grounded for a loooong time, also finish it.
- Try moving all your furniture around and redecorate your room *à la* Feng Shui.
- Learn to meditate.
- Do your Christmas card list and plan presents.
- Check out astrology sites on the Web and do friends' horoscopes for them.
- Treat the time as if you're at a health spa – give yourself a facial, paint your nails, condition your hair, moisturise and exfoliate.
- Exercise.
- Listen to music.
- Write music or lyrics.
- Learn to cook a new recipe (earns good brownie points if it comes out well and may get you time off for good behaviour)
- Clean the house and do the garden (also earns brownie points).
- Read. Some books are pretty cool and it's a way to escape from your personal prison into other worlds.

Chapter 8

Dragon Mother

Josh was already on a bench with his mates at Pond Square when I got there. I felt a bit intimidated as I approached, as I didn't know any of the others, but Josh soon waved me over and introduced me. There were two girls, Chris and Zoë, and a guy called Spider. They looked like they were in Year Eleven. Spider was the one who'd been chucking bread at passing joggers the week before and I didn't much like the look of him. He had very pale skin and was a bit hard-looking, but the girls seemed OK. They sized me up (girls can be a bit funny sometimes when you're not part of their group) and must have decided I was all right, because Chris rummaged in a carrier bag and pulled out a bottle of Malibu and a paper cup.

'Want some?'

'No thanks,' I said. 'I've got a band rehearsal later.'

'Oh, just have one. One won't hurt you.'

I didn't really want any, but I'd only just met them and I didn't want to be a killjoy when they were being friendly. Then I remembered what Tony said on the night of the cocktails. Lesson Number One: don't mix your drinks. That's probably why I'd felt so lousy. I'd mixed so many. Maybe if I'd just stuck to *one*, I'd have been OK. Then I remembered what Josh said about getting back on the horse after a bad experience. *Then* I remembered Angus saying never say never.

'OK. Thanks,' I said. I took the the cup she offered me.

I resolved not to overdo it as I could still remember how rotten I felt after the cocktails, so I stuck to my guns and I only had the one, even if Chris did fill the cup full. It tasted quite nice, coconutty, and I imagined it was probably nicer than the cider that Spider was drinking. I tried cider once at my stepsister's wedding and it tasted like apples that had gone off. Foul.

I sipped my Malibu and this time I felt OK. Somehow the drink made me feel more confident about being with strangers. I found myself feeling really talkative and told them all about King Noz and the gig on Saturday. They all seemed impressed and wanted to come along. At one point, my mobile rang, but I quickly switched it off. Probably Mum checking up on me, I thought.

'So do you rehearse often?' asked Chris.

'Yeah, we've done loads over the holidays,' I said, checking my watch. It wasn't until then that I realised what time it was. The rehearsal at Ben's was supposed to be at six and already it was a quarter past. 'Oh God,' I said and got up from the bench. 'Better get going.'

Josh walked with me to the High Street and just as I was about to dash off, he caught the back of my jacket, pulled me back and kissed me. Just like that. It took my breath away as it was so out of the blue. After a while, he let me go and we smiled at each other.

'Give me your number,' he said.

I scribbled it down on an old tube ticket that I had in my purse, then he gently pushed me down the road. 'You'd better get moving if you're going to go and be a rock chick fabster.'

'Not that kind of girl . . . or music,' I said, laughing, then ran like mad to get to Ben's on the other side of Highgate, down near the tube station. I felt totally exhilarated. He'd *kissed* me. No awkwardness. No build-up. No thinking, Is he going to? Isn't he? Should I kiss him? He'd done it when it was completely unexpected. It felt great. Sometimes getting that first kiss over with can be a bit clumsy.

When I got to Ben's, there was a note sellotaped to the garage door with my name on it. I ripped it open. '*Iz. Gone to check out the acoustics at the venue for Saturday. We waited for twenty minutes, then I tried your mobile, but it was switched off. Call me later. Ben.'*

Oh poo, I thought. I could have stayed longer in the square with Josh. I wondered if I should go back there, but decided it wouldn't look good. Nesta had drilled into all of us that it was important not to look too keen when you first meet a boy. I looked at my watch again. It was a quarter to seven. No way I felt like going home yet. Nesta's house was closest, but I couldn't go there as that's out of bounds for a while. I quickly called Lucy's. No one there, so I tried her mobile. She was at Nesta's. Oh, double poo, I thought. I can't risk the wrath of Dragon Mother if she finds out. At least TJ wasn't with them, so I called her. Luckily she was in, so I made my way over there.

I could see that something was wrong the moment TJ opened the door. She quickly ushered me upstairs into her bedroom and shut the door.

'Your mum's on the warpath,' she said. 'She's on her way over.'

'What? Why?'

TJ sat at her desk. 'Oh, some mix-up. She's been phoning everywhere. She said you were supposed to have been at Ben's. She rang there and his mum said you hadn't shown up for rehearsal, so the boys had gone off without you . . .'

I sank on to her bed. 'Hell's bells. I *did* go, but I went to Pond Square first.' I quickly filled TJ in on seeing Josh again and how fab it had been. 'But I don't believe it. She's checking up on me.'

At that moment, we heard a car drawing up outside. TJ peeked out the window. 'She's here. Look, if you had a drink, you'd better go and clean your teeth. She might smell it.'

'I only had one and it tasted like it was mainly coconut.'

'Breathe on me.'

I quickly breathed on TJ and we got the giggles as she fell back against the wall and feigned passing out.

'Smells slightly of alcohol,' she said. 'You'd better not risk it. Just rub some toothpaste on your teeth, then I'll give you some gum.'

I rushed into the bathroom and did as TJ had advised.

'Isobel, can you come down,' Scary Dad called up the stairs. 'Your mother's here.'

I had a quick gargle with some mouthwash as well for good measure, then combed my hair. TJ was waiting for me on the landing outside the bathroom. She looked really sorry for me. 'It'll be OK,' she said. 'Just tell them what happened.'

'You don't know my mum,' I said. 'She'd go ballistic if she knew I'd been hanging out with strangers.'

'Izzie.' This time it was Mum's voice and I knew I had no choice but to go down and face the firing squad.

★ ★ ★

Mum was deep in conversation with Scary Dad when we got downstairs. TJ and I stood there for what felt like hours before they acknowledged us. They seemed to have bonded over shock horror stories about alcohol abuse. I couldn't believe it. So much for keeping what happened at Nesta's private. She'd clearly told him all about it, and now anyone would think I was a regular drinker, the way they were going on and the looks they were giving me. Scary Dad works as a hospital consultant and was telling Mum about his early days when he worked in Accident and Emergency.

'You'd be surprised how many teenagers came in, vomit all over them, out of their minds . . .'

Mum was shaking her head. 'I know. Terrible, isn't it?'

I wanted to shout, '*But I'm not one of them!* I'm not *that* stupid,' but I just stood there like a lemon instead. TJ's dad is so intimidating. I just hoped that I hadn't got TJ in trouble with him, as he was even looking at *her* suspiciously.

Finally, Mum turned to me. 'Ah, there you are. And where do you think you've been?'

'Upstairs with TJ.'

'You told me that you had a rehearsal.'

'I did. But by the time I got there, the boys had gone.'

'And why were you late getting there?'

Talk about an inquisition, I thought. Why couldn't she wait until later? TJ and her dad didn't need to hear this.

'I . . . er, walked there.'

'Why? Why didn't you get the tube?'

'It was a nice evening . . .'

'So why did it take so long to walk? You must know how long it takes. You must have known you were going to be late if you walked. So *why* didn't you set off in time? And why didn't you phone when Ben wasn't there?'

'*Mum* . . .' I wished she'd stop. I glanced at TJ and Scary Dad. She looked uncomfortable and he looked like he was enjoying every minute. 'You knew I was going to be out for a while. I didn't think . . .' As I said this, Scary Dad and her exchanged weary, knowing looks. 'I . . . I came here instead.'

'We had an agreement, young lady. I said I wanted to know exactly where you were at every hour of the day.'

'You can always call. I have my mobile . . .'

She shook her head. 'Forget that. For one thing, you can turn it off and for another, I may phone you, but I still wouldn't really know where you were. You could tell me anything. No, from now on, I want the land-line number of where you are so that I can phone and check.'

TJ was looking at me with great sympathy. Her dad was looking at me as though I was a criminal. I wanted to die.

'*Why* couldn't you have waited?' I asked as soon as the car pulled away from TJ's. '*Why* did you have to do that in front of everyone?' I'd felt so humiliated, getting a public telling-off and I hadn't even *done* anything.

'You weren't where you said you were going to be,' said Mum through tight lips.

'Then please, I'm asking you from my heart, please, in future, wait until we're home or at least on our own before you yell at me. And I don't even know why you're so upset. Don't you trust me or something?'

'I don't think your recent behaviour has left that open for discussion, Izzie.'

'But I haven't *done* anything. It's not fair.'

'You don't think, Izzie.' Mum turned to look at me. 'I'm your mother and I don't know where you are any more. Or who you're hanging out with.'

'Well, I've been upstairs in my room for the last two days. You haven't had to look far. And you *do* know who I hang out with. TJ, Lucy, Nesta. Same as always.'

'Well, where were you tonight before Ben's.'

'I told you, walking to his house.'

'And what were you doing as you walked?'

'Nothing.'

'So why do you smell so strongly of toothpaste? Don't think I don't know all the tricks, Izzie.'

'TJ gave me a stick of gum, that's all.'

We drove a bit further in silence, then she piped up again. 'So who's the boy you were in the park with on Sunday?'

That shut me up for a moment. 'What boy?'

Mum hesitated for a moment. 'Mrs Peters next door said she saw you with a boy on Sunday in Primrose Hill park, on the night you were supposed to be coming straight home from your dad's.'

'I . . . I don't remember,' I said. 'Maybe I bumped into one of the boys from the band. I don't remember. And anyway, can't I even talk to people I know now?'

Mum saying Mrs Peters had seen me threw me for a moment. I didn't remember seeing her around when I was with Josh. The park was empty and she's not someone who's easy to miss as she's about eighteen stone. I decided to zip it. At least she hadn't seen me this evening, drinking and snogging.

'And what happened to you and Ben?' she asked. 'I thought you liked him.'

'I do,' I said. 'We're mates.' Why was she going on about this? I wondered. I hadn't told her that Ben and I had finished, but then I'd never told her that we were going out. It wasn't like we were engaged to be married or anything. It was way more casual. But how did she know we weren't having a relationship any more? Maybe she's more tuned into my life than I realised.

'So who's this boy in the park?'

She clearly wasn't going to let it go. 'Nobody.'

'What's his name?'

'Josh.'

'What school does he go to?'

'I *don't know*!'

'Don't raise your voice, Isobel. Where did you meet him?'

'Oh, just around.'

'And where does he live?'

'Dunno. I'm only just getting to know him.'

'Well, I'd like to meet him. Invite him over to the house.'

'*Whadt!*'

'You heard me. I like to know who you're spending time with.'

'But *Mum*, it's not like that. He's not like my *boy*friend. I *can't* invite him over. I hardly even *know* him.' This was appalling. Imagine me inviting Josh back and her giving him the third degree! She must be out of her mind. It was so unfair. She was ruining everything before it even got started.

'Bring him over one night at the weekend.'

'I *can't*, Mum.'

'Why not? If he's a friend, surely he must know you have parents.'

'Yes, but . . . *no*. Oh, you don't understand.' She didn't. I could *never* in a million squillion years invite the coolest boy I'd ever met back to meet my dragon of a mother. Especially as we hadn't even been on a date. He'd run a mile if I asked him.

'If you don't bring him back, I don't want you to see him.'

'But you never met Ben in the early days.'

'Yes, but I knew who he was and I know he goes to the same school as Lucy's brothers. And I know where he lives as I've dropped you off there a few times.' Then she smiled. 'I really think that you're making a fuss about nothing, Izzie. It's no big deal. Just invite him back for half an hour or so. I promise I'll be very nice to him. I just want to meet him, that's all.'

Sometimes life really sucks, I thought, as we drove on. No big deal? Maybe not if you're living in Jane Austen's times, but it is if you live in North London in the twenty-first century.

Song for Nagging Mothers
You're So Rotten

You're always telling me to do things like you do.
You're always saying my room looks like a zoo.
Well, I don't care. So there.
You're always telling me that you don't like my
mood.
You're always complaining that my friends are rude.
Well, I don't care. So there.

I really hate you, yes I do.
I really hate you, yes I do.
Do I really hate you?
Yes I do.

You never listen to the things I gotta say.
Whenever I need you, you turn and walk away.
Well, I don't care. So there.
I'm so angry, yes I am.
I'm so angry, yes I am.
Am I really angry?
You bet I stinking am.
So there. I don't care.

I really hate you, yes I do.
I really hate you, yes I do.
Do I really hate you?
Yes I do.

Chapter 9

War

I don't believe it. I *really* don't believe it! Mum has read my diary!

It was obvious as soon as I got back to my bedroom and went to get it out. It had been moved from its place in my underwear drawer. I always kept it under the Calvin Klein pants that my stepsiter Amelia gave me. They're a size too big, so I never wear them. Now the diary was under a white T-shirt and I'd never have put it there. How *could* she? I thought, as I grabbed it and stormed downstairs.

Mum was sitting in the living room, having a drink with Angus. I could tell that they'd been talking about me by the way they suddenly went silent and looked guilty when I burst in. I stood by Mum's chair and pointed at my diary.

'Mrs Peter never was in the park, was she?'

For once in her life, Mum looked sheepish.

'How *could* you, Mum?' I asked. 'This is really, *really* private.'

Angus got up and tiptoed out behind me.

Mum looked at the carpet. 'Well, how else am I supposed to know what's going on with you? You never talk to me about your life and I've been worried about you lately.'

'But reading my *diary* . . .' I felt near to tears. I wrote *all* sorts of stuff in my diary, mad stuff, thoughts, feelings. It was a way of unloading, and often the way I felt one day was different the next. It wasn't meant to be seen by anyone and it was *horrible* to think that someone had read it. I felt totally exposed, like I was naked.

'Come and sit down, Izzie. Let's talk about this . . .'

I turned and headed back up the stairs. I had nothing more to say to her. If she's done this, I thought, then she clearly has no idea of who I really am and certainly doesn't trust me. There's only one thing for it, I decided. I'll go to my room, put a chair in front of the door so that no one can get in, and tomorrow first thing, I'm going to go live with Dad.

'Hello, love,' said Dad as he opened the door the next morning and looked at his watch. 'You're here early. I was just off to college.'

I hauled my bag up the steps to his flat and into the hall. 'I wanted to catch you before you left. Can I come and live here with you and Anna? I'll sleep on the sofa bed and I won't be any trouble, I just can't take it at home any more. It's been awful lately and she's gone too far this time. She's driving me mad.'

'Whoa, slow down, slow down,' said Dad. 'Come into the kitchen and tell me all about it.'

I followed him in and blurted out everything that had happened over the last few days. 'I really can't stay there any longer,' I said finally. 'She's a monster. I quite understand why you divorced her.'

Dad smiled sadly. 'She's not a monster, Izzie, she's just . . . oh dear, Izzie, what are we to do?' He glanced at his watch. 'I've got a lecture in half an hour, so I can't get into all this now, but listen . . . I agree your mum should never have read your diary, but, as for walking out on her . . . you know she has your best interests at heart . . .'

'But she doesn't seem to realise that I'm not a little girl who needs constant looking after any more . . .' My voice trailed off. I knew that he was going to tell me to go back. Part of me had been expecting it anyway, as I knew they didn't really have room. I sat at the table and put my head in my hands.

'You have a nice home there,' Dad continued, 'and your own room. It would drive you mad here, not having your own space. You know that's true.'

'Can't I just stay a few days?'

Dad sighed. 'You're always welcome, Izzie, but . . . where would we put you? Anna's mum and dad are arriving from Scotland this evening and will be staying for a couple of days. Anna and I are going to give them our bedroom and we're going to camp on the sofa bed in the front room with Tom. So where would we put you? Listen, love, let me call your mum to let her know that you're here, then stay until I get back at lunchtime and we'll talk about it some more. I'll drive you back and I'll have a chat with her and see what we can work out.'

'Promise?'

'Promise.'

Mum clearly wasn't in the chatting mood. It was horrible. Dad had only been in the house five minutes when they got into a huge argument about responsibility. She was coming out with the same old stuff about it being her who lay awake at night worrying about me. I couldn't bear it, so I slipped into Angus's study to hide until it was all over.

After a few minutes, I heard the front door open. I peeked out and spotted Angus coming back with a sandwich for his lunch. He cocked an ear at the kitchen door, then when he realised what was going on, he turned on his heel and dived into the study, closing the door firmly behind him.

Then he saw me.

'Hiding?'

I nodded.

'Good idea. Don't blame you,' he said. 'Best to lie low

in here until it all blows over.' He offered me half of his sandwich. 'Cheese and tomato?'

I shook my head and sat on the floor by the bookshelves. I felt miserable. Dad didn't want me at his house and I didn't want to live here. I didn't belong anywhere.

Angus looked at me with concern. 'Been having a tough old time lately, haven't you?'

I felt tears prick the back of my eyes. I blinked to make them go away. The last thing I wanted to do was cry in front of Angus. But too late. He'd seen and was handing me a tissue.

'There, there,' he said. 'Have a good old blow.'

I blew my nose into the tissue, but it didn't help. Tears were spilling out of my eyes and down my cheeks. I pointed at the door. We could still hear raised voices in the kitchen. 'I didn't mean this to happen. I didn't mean any of it to happen. Just . . . everything seems to be going wrong lately. Everything I touch turns into a disaster. Mum doesn't understand me and now I've caused a row between her and Dad . . . What's wrong with me?'

Angus chuckled. 'Nothing. You're a teenager.'

'I bet Claudia and Amelia never did anything wrong,' I said. More perfect girls you could never hope to meet. Both polite, both in good jobs, both married to accountants.

Angus laughed out loud and got up and went to one of

his shelves. 'Those two girls made my life a living hell,' he said. 'Want to see some pictures of them in their punk days?'

'*Punk* days? Amelia and Claudia? Never!' My stepsisters were straighter than straight – blonde, tidy, the kind of girls who looked like they never had a bad hair day.

Angus passed me the album. Two girls with wild black hair and a ton of black eye make-up stared defiantly out from the photographs, Amelia with the full spiked-up works, Claudia in a tiny kilt, rubber basque and chains. Both had green lipstick on. Underneath the photos, Angus had written, 'Insanity is hereditary. You get it from your kids.'

I burst out laughing. '*Excellent.*' That's one for Lucy's slogan collection, I thought. She spent the summer making T-shirts with cool slogans on them and had asked us all to keep our eyes out for good lines.

Angus shook his head. 'It got to a point where my wife and I were afraid to go away for fear of what they might get up to in our absence. One time, half the neighbourhood came for a party and trashed the place – motorbikes on the lawn, police cars at midnight . . .'

'I'm stunned,' I said as I stared at the photos and thought about the girls now. One a lawyer, the other an accountant, neat and demure in their Jasper Conran outfits. Both had homes with matching towels in the bathroom . . .

'So was I,' said Angus. 'It took me *years* to recover.'

'Looking at these, I can't help but think, so what's Mum's problem, then? I mean, no offence, but I've never been this wild.'

Angus sat at his desk. 'Your mum cares deeply about you, Izzie. You must know that. I know you've got to grow up and be independent, but you'll always be her little girl, just as Amelia and Claudia will always be my little girls, whatever age they are. Don't forget a few years ago, you were all cuddles and wanting to be with her. It can be hard — suddenly she's being shoved away as you want to be more adult and make your own choices. It's a difficult time of adjustment for parents as well. I remember when my two didn't want to hug me any more. If I ever went to embrace them, they'd push me away. And if I ever went to pick them up from anywhere, I was asked to stay out of sight round a corner because they were ashamed of me. They didn't want to be associated with an old fogey like me. I was out of date. Only years before, they were a pair of real daddy's girls. I was their hero, they followed me everywhere. Then suddenly, they didn't need or want me any more. The rejection was tough to take.'

I flicked through his album, taking in pictures of the girls as babies, then toddlers, then eight, nine, ten, holding their mum and dad's hands, smiling at the camera. Then they turned into a pair of sulky teenagers with dyed hair and mad clothes.

'I guess,' I said. I'd never thought about parents feeling rejected before. To me, Mum was just Mum, always there. But I suppose I had shut her out lately and there was a time when we used to hang out together a lot. And it was true, I couldn't even remember the last time I gave her a hug. 'Hmmm.' I smiled at Angus. 'How about you talk to her? She *can* trust me, you know. Just ask her to chill out a bit.'

'I will. Of course I will. Just try to meet her halfway,' said Angus. 'I bet you'll find that it makes a world of difference. Now, how about half that sarnie while the cast of *EastEnders* finish fighting it out in the kitchen.'

I took the sandwich this time. 'Thanks, Angus.'

He smiled. 'You're welcome, Izzie.'

After talking to Angus, I went to my room and ripped up the song I'd written about hating Mum so much. In the light of what Angus had said, it seemed really harsh, and although I was mad with her at the time, I would have hated for her to ever find it and think that I really meant it. Writing it was just a way of letting off steam. I guess I've got to find a way to express the times when she doesn't wind me up as well, I thought.

As I was ripping the sheet of paper into tiny pieces, I heard the front door open and close. I looked out the window to see Dad leaving. He looked up at me, smiled and gave me the thumbs-up. Phew, at least that's over, I thought as minutes later I heard his car drive away.

Moments later, I heard Mum's footsteps on the stairs. I took a deep breath and resolved to be nice to her. It wasn't hard when she came in, as she looked strained after the conversation with Dad. I was sorry I put her through it.

'Er, Izzie . . .' she began.

'Me first,' I said. 'I want to say I'm sorry for . . . er, taking off this morning. It's not that I don't appreciate everything you do and I know you worry about me and I'll try harder in future not to upset you.'

Mum's face relaxed and she sat on the end of my bed. 'Did you really want to leave and live at your dad's?'

'Not really,' I lied. I'd love to live at Dad's, if there was room, but I wasn't going to tell her that. 'I don't think I'd last a day without my own space. I'm sorry I put you through that.'

'Me too. I'm sorry we haven't been getting along lately. I can't help worrying about you, but I'll try not to be too much of an over-anxious mother. So, what are you going to do this afternoon? Oh . . .' She laughed. 'I'm not checking up on you, only asking . . .'

I laughed as well. 'I may do some homework,' I said. 'And I may go up to Muswell Hill to get some things from Ryman's that I need for school – if that's OK. Do you want me to call you from Muswell Hill?'

Mum looked up at the ceiling and smiled. 'No. I trust you to go to the stationery shop. Honestly. Am I really so bad?' She glanced at the clock. 'Oh . . . got to dash. They'll be wondering where I am at work, wandering off in the middle of the day . . .'

'Sorry about that,' I said, looking at the carpet. I did feel a bit ashamed. I'd caused chaos today – Dad having to leave college and Mum having to come home from work on her lunch hour.

Mum looked at me with concern. 'So, are we all right now?'

I nodded.

She looked at her watch again. '*Oh*. Got to go. Oh, and . . . I'll be back late tonight. There's a work's function I can't avoid. It's such a nuisance, these dinners always come at the most inconvenient times. I'd rather come back and have a proper chat about things, but it's not something I can get out of. Angus will be coming with me, so . . . will you be all right on your own this evening? These things tend to go on a bit. I might not be back until it's gone midnight. I can ask Angus to stay if you like. He doesn't really need to be there.'

'No, don't be silly. Go. Have a good time. I don't need babysitting.'

'Only if you're sure.'

'I'm fine, Mum. And we can chat another time,' I said, feeling slightly relieved. Then I put on a stern expression. 'And if you're going to be in past midnight, I expect a call. I lie awake worrying if you're not in.'

Mum raised an eyebrow in surprise. 'Don't push it,' she said as she went out the door. But she was smiling.

At last, everything's back to normal, I thought after she'd gone.

But there are twenty-four hours in a day and Thursday wasn't over yet.

Line for Lucy's T-shirt Collection

Insanity is hereditary.
You get it from your kids.

Chapter 10

Best and Worst

The following day, I decided to do the exercise that we'd been set for the holidays. I'd been putting it off all summer, so, with only three days left before school started, I thought I'd better make an effort.

Our teacher, Miss Watkins, had given us the opening lines to the book *A Tale of Two Cities* by Charles Dickens.

I picked up the handout sheet and read:

> *It was the best of times, it was the worst of times, it was the age of wisdom, it was the age of foolishness, it was the epoch of belief, it was the epoch of incredulity, it was the season of Light, it was the season of Darkness, it was the spring of hope, it was the winter of despair, we had everything before us, we*

had nothing before us, we were all going direct to Heaven, we were all going direct the other way.

Boy, he sounds confused, I thought, up and down and round and round. Seems like some things never change. Then I looked to see what we were meant to do with the handout. Miss Watkins had written underneath the quote: *'Write a short account of the best and worst times of your summer.'* Forget the *whole* summer, I thought, as I sat as my desk, I could put them all into one day: yesterday.

I got a few sheets of paper out of my desk drawer and began to write:

Worst: *being mad with Mum and storming off to Dad's only to find out that staying with him was a no-go.*

Best: *my talk with Angus. I'm beginning to really like him. Then everything being OK between Mum and me again.*
Josh phoned an hour after Mum had gone back to her office. He wanted to meet up, so I suggested Muswell Hill as I'd already told Mum I was going there.

Worst: *went to meet Josh. It was pouring. Not gentle summer rain, this was torrential. Arrived looking like a drowned rat. So much for looking cool. I was positively frozen.*

Best: *Josh was soaked too and looked drop-dead gorgeous with wet hair slicked back and his skin glistening with rain. He put* *his arm around me as we ran through the downpour, then kissed me under a tree. Possibly the most romantic moment of my whole life, even though water was dripping down the back of my jacket.*

Worst: *met up with his weird friend Spider. Don't like him. He is Sullen with a capital S. Josh did ask if I minded hooking up with him. Actually, I did mind, as I wanted to get to know Josh better, but then I remembered what happened to Lucy this summer. She went out with this guy who was really clingy and possessive. He started telling her who she could and couldn't see, and in the end, she finished with him because she felt suffocated. Didn't want to do that to Josh.*

Worst: *had a cigarette. Spider offered me one and I took it. I don't know why. I guess I wanted to look cool. Hah. I took one puff and blaghh, I gagged on it. Spider creased up laughing. Won't be trying one of those again in a hurry, as it tasted disgusting. Josh had one as well and when he kissed me afterwards, it wasn't as nice as before in the rain. He had cigarette-breath. But I guess I did too. Should have taken some gum.*

Best: *Josh held my hand as we walked along in the rain. It made me feel like he was happy to be seen with me.*

Worst: *made huge mistake and took Josh and Spider to Ben's* garage. I knew it was empty, as Ben had gone to his gran's eightieth birthday in Brighton with his family and wouldn't be back until late. I guess I wanted to impress Josh, but it backfired. I knew it wasn't a good idea the moment we got there. Spider had been drinking and carried on drinking. He was into everything, opening drawers and picking up the guitars. I had to tell him to leave them alone, as the boys are very picky about who handles their instruments and don't like people messing with them. Then he started pulling CDs and things out of Ben's filing cabinet. I know he has everything dated and labelled, so had to tell Spider to get lost. In the end I asked him to leave. He told me not to get my knickers in a twist. Very original. Not. After he'd gone, Josh lay on the sofa, rolling joints. Got a bit worried that Ben would smell marijuana when he got back. Josh said that marijuana is nicer than tobacco, so I had a quick puff. He told me that I had to really inhale it, which I did and it made my head go woozy. Not sure that I liked the sensation.

Best: listening to music, talking and snogging Josh on the sofa. I give him nine out of ten on the snogging scale. Minus one because I could taste the tobacco and an aphrodisiac it is definitely not.

Worst: after we left the garage and I locked up, it was ten-forty. I knew Mum wouldn't be home until after midnight, so no worries there, but I knew I shouldn't get back any later. Josh *said he was off to a party and when I said I couldn't go, he was like, Oh, OK, I'll give you a call, then. Then off he went, leaving me standing there on the pavement. Felt confused, as after all that snogging, I thought he'd at least care about how I got home. Didn't like being out on my own so late at night. Phoned Nesta as she was closest and she and Tony came and escorted me home. Tony was very sniffy about Josh. He said that he thought Josh sounded like a creep and any boy should always make sure a girl gets home safe as there are too many weirdos about. Nesta thinks I shouldn't see Josh, as he sounds like bad news. Felt very confused. I don't know whether she's right or whether she's jealous because she thought he was cute in the beginning, but he never gave her any attention.*

I looked over what I had written for my best and worst, then ripped it up and threw it in the bin. Somehow I don't think Miss Watkins would be too happy if she knew I'd been drinking, smoking, puffing on joints and snogging boys. I tried to rethink what Dickens had said in the light of what had happened to me.

I wrote:

It was the best of times, it was the worst of times. It was the age of Year Ten, it was the age of growing up. It was a time of discovery. It was a time of being silly. It was an era of fighting with my mum. It was an era of trying to accept her. It was the season of rebellion, then the season of regret. The spring of new love, the winter of disappointment. I had a new boyfriend, I didn't have a new boyfriend. I was going direct to romance, I was going direct home, alone to bed.

Yeah, I thought. Times haven't changed much at all since Dickens lived. Life is still a rollercoaster. Opposites. Good times, bad times, best and worst. I wondered how the rest of my class was getting on with the exercise and how their summers had been. It would be hysterical if everyone wrote the truth about what we'd got up to, as knowing the girls in our year, they'll have been up to all sorts.

As I tried to get into writing the more socially acceptable version of my best and worst times, Lucy phoned.

'Oh, I've done that homework,' she said. 'Took two minutes. Best time: breaking up for the summer holidays. Worst time: well, that will be going back on Monday, won't it?'

I laughed. 'I guess. Might be a bit short for what's expected, though.'

'I'll tell her I'm going through a minimalist phase with my writing. Less is more sort of thing. Anyway, forget about homework, we'll have enough of that soon when term starts and if you ever get stuck, Lal has been working on a list of good excuses for handing homework in late. He's hoping TJ will put it in the magazine, but I don't think she'll dare. He'll e-mail it to you, if you like. But tell me all about Josh. Nesta said you saw him yesterday. What's he really like?'

'Weird,' I said, 'or maybe not weird. More like

mysterious. He's quite unlike anyone I've ever met before. I don't feel I know him at all. Like, I asked him where he lived and he said, "Planet Earth." I asked him what school he went to and he said, "The school of life." I asked him what birth sign he was, as I thought I could do a horoscope to see if we're compatible. He said, "Marsupian."'

Lucy laughed. 'Marsupian. At least he didn't say he was from Uranus.'

'I even tried your quiz, Lucy. You know, the one about your three favourite animals and why?'

'What did he say?'

'First, he went a bit funny and asked if it was one of those girlie magazine quizzes on how to pigeonhole a boy. Then he said, "Number one: Bugs Bunny because he's got big furry feet. Number two: Shrek from the movie because he's green and rubbery. And number three: a Teletubby because although they're not real animals, they're sure as hell not human."'

'So he wasn't taking it seriously?'

'He doesn't seem to take anything seriously,' I said, and I told her about him leaving me to get home on my own.

'That's sucks,' said Lucy. 'Bin him.'

'Do you think?'

'Definitely. He may be gorgeous and different, but I think it's really uncool for a boy to leave a girl stranded on the street when it's late.'

'That's what Tony said.'

'Plus, the way he evaded giving you any information about himself,' she continued. 'It seems like he won't let you get too close. All those jokey answers. I've heard Mum talk about clients who do that. She says people use humour as a block or defence sometimes.'

Lucy's mum works as a counsellor. She's really cool and has good insight into people. She was certainly right about Josh. It was like he was shielding me off. I knew nothing about him and he knew everything about me, as I'd answered his questions truthfully.

'You deserve better,' said Lucy.

'But he *is* a good kisser . . .'

'So? So are lots of boys.'

'You're right. And I did feel crapola standing on the street after he took off last night. Sort of like I'd been discarded when my use ran out. Yeah, from this moment on, Josh is Izzie history.'

Excuses for Handing in Homework Late
By Lal Lovering

- My homework is late because I was up all night writing letters demanding better pay for teachers.
- Aliens from the planet Zog took my homework as an example of great Earth literature.
- I can't give in my homework as we had burglars last night and they stole it.
- I couldn't do my homework because I accidentally superglued my teeth together and had to go to the dentist's.
- I can't hand in my homework because the cat had kittens in my schoolbag.
- I've been replaced by an evil robot replica and it doesn't do homework.
- I couldn't do my homework because my contact lenses stuck to my eyes.
- I couldn't do my homework because I was grieving the death of my pet rock.
- I have done my homework, but it's done in invisible ink.
- My homework's late because I have an attention deficient disorder, er . . . what was I saying?
- I didn't do my homework because my inner child didn't feel like it.

Chapter 11

Turnaround

I was woken the next day by a frantic phone call from Ben. 'Izzie, have you by any chance taken the CD with the songs we're going to do tonight? Remember, I recorded it a few weeks ago when we had that run-through?'

I did remember. It was a good session and everyone was in a really good mood, playing well and in tune. There was a possibility that a talent scout might be at the gig tonight and Ben wanted to be ready with a demo CD to give him.

'I've looked everywhere,' Ben continued. 'And I've spoken to the other lads. No one's seen it.'

I felt my stomach churn. I had a feeling that I knew *exactly* where it was. Spider. He must have taken it last night.

'No, I haven't got it, Ben,' I said. 'Haven't you got another copy?'

'No. I was going to do some today. Never mind. It's got to be here somewhere. I'll carry on looking.'

I felt rotten when I put the phone down, but I just couldn't bring myself to tell him that I'd taken two boys back to the garage. Even though we're not an item any more, I didn't want to hurt his feelings. I'll kill Spider, I thought. I have to get the CD back, but then I'm not going to see Josh again, am I? So how am I going to see Spider? Luckily the phone went again and this time it was Josh. He asked if I'd meet him in Highgate. My first reaction was to say no, as I still felt bad after being abandoned last night, but I wanted to get the CD back from Spider in time for the gig, plus I wanted to get something for Mum's birthday tomorrow, so in the end, I agreed.

I set off for Highgate, thinking that I'd be really cool with Josh this time. I'd ask how I could get the CD back and I'd let him know that he couldn't just see me when he chose, then abandon me when he had a better offer.

He was waiting for me in Costa on the High Street at a table at the back. I sat opposite him and resolved that I wasn't going to gabble away and do all the talking. If he was going to be mysterious, then so was I.

'Hi,' he said.

'Hi.'

He looked up at me, then down at the floor and shifted

uncomfortably. He fumbled in his jacket pocket. 'First of all, let me give you this back.' He handed me Ben's CD. 'I wanted to hear what your band sounded like. I know I should have told you, but I know a few people in bands and it can be so embarrassing if they're rotten and you have to fake what you think. I wanted to listen to you in private. It's good. Genuinely. And you have a great voice, Izzie. Real talent.'

'Thanks. I . . .'

'And second,' he interrupted. 'I was a real shit last night and I want to apologise. I shouldn't have left you on your own . . .'

My jaw dropped. This wasn't what I expected.

'So sorry,' he continued. 'I don't know why I did it. It's weird sometimes with girls. It's like . . . I dunno, like when I really like someone, sometimes it does my head in and I cut off. I know it's mad . . .' He shifted in his seat again. 'Plus things have been crap at home, you know, lot going on . . .'

'Tell me about it,' I said. 'I seem to have been in the doghouse all summer. So what's happening at home?'

Josh hesitated. 'Oh, the usual – parents, school, exams, life,' he said finally.

'Yeah. Same ole, same ole,' I said. 'Do you have brothers and sisters?'

Josh shook his head. 'Just me.'

'So what's been the problem?'

Josh hesitated again. 'It's my dad, really . . .' He seemed reluctant to carry on, so I reached over, took his hand and squeezed it.

'You don't have to tell me if you don't want,' I said.

Josh shrugged. 'No, it's not that I don't want to tell you, just that a lot of people don't want to know when they find out what my dad does.'

'Why? What does he do?'

Josh glanced around him, then sighed. 'Let's just put it this way: he spends a lot of his time in police stations.'

Even though I tried to look cool about it, I think my face must have registered surprise. Josh scanned my face for a reaction, so I gave him a sympathetic smile as if to say, what his dad did wasn't going to put me off him.

'Ever since I was a kid,' he continued, 'I never really knew what my dad was up to. Out nights, didn't know where he'd been when he finally did come home. And the stress it causes my mum – the atmosphere at home is rotten. She wants him to get a normal job, live a normal life, but nah, what can you do?'

'Oh, I'm so sorry, Josh. It must be hard having a dad who's been inside . . .' I began.

'Inside?' Suddenly he grinned as though he found it funny. 'Yeah. My dad's a right dodgy geezer, but once someone's turned rotten, you can't change them.' Suddenly, his expression changed to sadness. Ah, I thought, so that's it. His devil-may-care attitude is a cover for how he really feels. Poor Josh. It must be awful having a dad who's in and out of prison.

'I try and keep out of his way as much as I can,' said Josh. 'Not that he's got much time for me. All he cares about is the latest job he's on. That's why I don't like going home much. I don't want to get into it or know what he's up to.'

'Where do you live?'

He jerked his thumb north. 'Up near Whetstone. But I tell you, I'm off the minute I can leave. I'll find a way to support myself. I mean, who wants to live somewhere where your dad's dodgy and your mum is paranoid that you're going to end up the same way. Like, I didn't get the grades I needed in my GCSEs this summer and now she's convinced I'm going the same way as my dad and won't get off my case. It's hell.'

I put my hand over his. 'I'm really sorry. I haven't been getting on with my mum lately either.'

'Yeah, but I don't think my dad even likes me. He's always picking on me, then mum stands up for me, then they start rowing. I mean, I've no intention of ending up like Dad – no way.'

He looked so vulnerable sitting there that I desperately wanted to make him feel better. All my resolve not to get involved went flying out the window. I felt the total opposite of how I felt last night. Then I'd felt used and discarded, now I felt needed. He was confiding in me and

I wanted to show him that I was there for him. He lit up a cigarette and offered me one.

I took one and told him I'd have it later.

'Want to hear something funny?' I asked.

He nodded.

'I wrote something about meeting you in my diary and my mum read it. She said she wants to meet you. As if.'

He looked chuffed. 'You wrote about me in your diary? What did you write?'

'None of your business.'

He laughed. 'I hope it was flattering.'

'Might have been. You'll never know.'

He looked at me seriously. 'I will come and meet her, if you like.'

I shook my head. 'No, don't be mad. She's just being over-protective. Worrying that I'm seeing some maniac.'

'I'm good with mums,' he said. 'Honest. I can be very charming when I want to be.'

'I'm sure you can, but no, forget it.'

'Oh, come on, it'll be a laugh. I can tell her all about how I want to be a doctor when I leave school.'

'You never told me that . . .'

He laughed. 'I have no intention of being a doctor, but that's the sort of thing mums like to hear.'

'So, you're good at telling women what they like to hear, are you?' I teased.

Josh shrugged, then laughed again. 'Yeah. Sometimes all

you have to do is feed them a line. They hear what they want to hear and run with it. Anyway, the offer's there and if it gets your mum off your back, then why not? It would also mean we could see each other without her giving you any hassle.'

That made sense. 'OK,' I said. 'But I'm warning you. She can be major inquisitive.'

'No problemo. So, you all ready for tonight?'

I nodded. 'Sort of, but I always feel a little nervous just before.'

'So how about I come over this evening before the gig and help you chill. We could go together.'

On the way home, I put the cigarette that Josh had given me in the bin, then quickly called in at Ben's. No one was there, so I posted the CD through the letter box with a note saying, *'Sorry, found this in my bag. Must have picked it up by mistake. Sorry, sorry. See you later.'*

Phew, that's sorted, I thought, heading home to meet Lucy. She was coming over to help me put my outfit together for the gig, plus I wanted to look good for Josh. I was glad he was the one who had taken the CD, as I wouldn't have liked a confrontation with Spider and I felt flattered that Josh had wanted to hear what I sounded like with the band. He was different today, I thought, as I walked towards the tube station. All his defences were down and I realised that he's as insecure as the rest of us. It must be rotten for him. Even though Mum and I have been at war lately, I know that she's there for me in her own uptight way. I decided I'd give her a hug when I got home.

She was in the kitchen making a sandwich when I got in, so I went over to her and put my arm around her waist.

'Hey, Mum,' I said. 'Had a good morning?'

'You've been smoking,' she said pulling back.

'No, I haven't,' I said.

Mum sighed. 'I can smell it, Izzie. In your hair.'

'I've been in a place where people were smoking, but I didn't. I don't even like cigarettes.'

'So you *have* tried one, then?'

'*No*. Yes, well only a puff, but never again. They stink.'

'What is it with you lately, Izzie? Drinking, smoking. Hanging out with strange boys. What next?'

How can parents switch moods so fast? I wondered. Last night she was being so nice before she went out and now, she's back on my case. It's so unfair. I don't smoke. I *won't* smoke. I try something and make a decision that she'd approve of and still I'm in the doghouse.

'Life is about making choices, Mum. To make choices, you have to know what's on offer. I did try a cigarette and I've decided not to smoke. Everyone my age tries one at some time or other.'

'But some choices are dangerous, Izzie. What else are you going to try?'

'Give me a break, Mum. I know what not to mess with.'

'Do you? *Do* you? How do I know that?' she said as she took a seat at the table. 'You're still young, Izzie. You need my protection.'

'Protection, yes. Suffocation, no.' I was starting to feel annoyed. Then I remembered what Angus had said about how watching your daughter grow up can be a difficult time of readjustment for parents. Slow down, I told myself. Be patient and meet her halfway.

'Mum, you *can* trust me.'

'I hope so, Izzie, because . . .'

'Oh, and that strange boy,' I interrupted. 'His name's Josh. He lives in Whetstone and he said he'd love to meet you. He's coming over this evening.'

Ha. That shut her up.

Line for Lucy's T-shirt Collection

As ye smoke, so shall ye reek

Chapter 12

The Big Night

True to his word, Josh arrived on my doorstep early evening, carrying a bunch of flowers. I was feeling really good, as Lucy had popped over earlier as promised and we'd put together an amazing outfit for the gig. She'd lent me a black corset-type basque that she'd made. It had criss-cross laces at the back, was low at the front and looked great with my tight black jeans and high boots. Nesta lent me a black beaded choker and I did my make-up darker than normal. When I'd finished, I thought the whole effect looked very rock-chick and cool.

Josh let out a long whistle when I opened the door. 'Whoa, you look *amazing*,' he said, looking me up and down. Then he laughed and indicated his jeans and fleece.

'And look at me, dressed all safe and normal, ready to meet Mummy dearest.'

'You look great,' I said, then I showed him into the hall. He *did* look good – even out of his usual bike leathers, he still gave off a vibe like he was all coiled up with energy, raring to go. And so sweet, he'd brought me flowers.

'Those for me?' I asked, pointing at the flowers.

He shook his head. 'For your mum.' Then he whispered, 'From the garden on the corner of your road.'

At that moment, Mum came out of the kitchen. She looked a bit shocked when she saw me, but didn't say anything. Instead she focused on Josh and shook his hand. 'So you're Josh,' she said.

He smiled back at her. 'And you must be one of Izzie's stepsisters.'

'No. I'm Izzie's mother,' she replied, and I could swear that her cheeks coloured a little.

'No way,' he said, handing her the flowers. 'You don't look old enough.'

Mum raised an eyebrow as though she didn't believe a word of it, then she laughed. 'Izzie never told me that you were so charming. Now, what can I get you?'

Cigarette and a can of lager, I thought, knowing Josh. But he just asked if she had Earl Grey tea.

'That's my favourite too,' she said, heading back for the kitchen. 'I'll bring it up to you. Izzie, do you want anything?'

'No, no, let me help you,' said Josh, following her, then turning back and giving me a conspiratorial wink.

I had to ring Ben to confirm a few last minute arrangements for the gig, so I left them to it in the kitchen. As I dialled Ben's number on the phone in the hall, I heard Mum laughing at something Josh said. Boy, he really is good with mums, I thought.

Over tea, he and Mum got to talking about his career. Anyone would think he's a prospective husband, the way she's sizing him up, I thought, as she asked about his aims and ambitions in life. He didn't seem to mind, though, and chatted away happily about plans for college. He even did the 'I may study to be a doctor' schpiel.

'Come on, Josh,' I said after Mum had plied him with cakes and biscuits. 'I'll show you my room.'

'And you must come and have supper with us one night,' said Mum. 'I'm sure my husband would like to meet you as well.'

'That would be great,' said Josh, getting up.

Once we got upstairs, I showed him my room, then quickly went to the bathroom. The pre-gig nerves were beginning to kick in and even though I've performed a number of times before, I still get jittery inside. When I went back into my bedroom, Josh was hanging out of the window, smoking a cigarette.

'*Hey*, don't do that in here,' I said, closing the door in a panic. 'Mum will kill me.'

'She won't smell it,' said Josh. 'I'm smoking it out the window.'

'You don't know my mum. She has the nose of a sniffer dog,' I said and quickly lit a joss stick, then sprayed the room with vanilla room spray. Josh stubbed out his cigarette and threw himself back on my bed. It felt so weird to actually have him there in my room, lying on *my* bed. If I was to choose an animal for how others see him, I thought, it would be a panther. Lean, beautiful and ready to pounce. Suddenly I felt awkward. I didn't know where to put myself or how to act. I think Josh was well aware off the effect he was having on me, and he caught my hand and pulled me down beside him just as there was a knock at the door.

'Izzie,' called Mum. 'Can I have a word?'

I sprang away from Josh and gave the room another spray. Oh poo, I thought. Is it because I closed the door when I've a boy in my room or because she's smelled the smoke. I went out into the corridor and shut the door behind me.

'Yes, Mum?'

She beckoned me into her bedroom.

'Close the door,' she said once we'd got inside.

Oh dear, she definitely smelled the cigarette, I thought, as I shut the door. What a shame, after it was all going so well.

'I've taken on board what you asked the other night about not saying things to you in front of people, so . . .'

'It wasn't me smoking,' I started.

'What do you mean? Smoking?' she asked, looking puzzled.

'Um, er, didn't you . . . I mean . . . Why is it you wanted to see me?'

'*Have* you been smoking in your room?'

'No. *No*. Course not.'

'Because I won't tolerate it if you have.'

'I told you I don't smoke.'

'So what are you talking about, then? Is Josh smoking in there?'

'No,' I said. It was the truth. He wasn't smoking in my room. At least, not any more. 'Mum. What is it you wanted?'

Mum looked at my outfit. 'I can't let you go out looking like that,' she said. 'That basque you've got on is too provocative. It gives out a message to boys, plus you've got far too much make-up on for someone your age.'

'But I'm performing, Mum. On *stage*. Not going shopping in Tesco's. I have to make an effort.'

'Just wipe a bit of it off,' she said. 'Your eyes are too heavy and that lipstick's too strong.'

'Fine,' I said. 'I'll wipe it off. Can I go now?'

'Yes, but please don't be sulky about it. I bet that nice young man of yours would agree with me. Most men prefer girls to look natural.'

'Yes, fine. Whatever,' I said, heading for the door.

'No, Izzie, I *mean* it. Find something else to wear or you're not going.'

'I'll wear my velvet top. OK?' I said, thinking that the sooner Josh and I get out of here, the better. And I knew I'd better act compliant as I was about to tell her something else. 'Oh . . . and Josh said he'll give me a ride on the back of his bike, so you don't need to drop me.'

'Bike? What bike?'

'Motorbike.'

'No, Izzie. I'm not letting you go on the back of one of those things. They're dangerous. I'll drop you and Mrs Lovering will pick you up. I spoke to her earlier and it's all arranged. And eat something before you go. I left a sandwich downstairs for you, as you'll miss supper.'

'I'm really not hungry, Mum. I can never eat before a gig.'

'Then take it with you and have it later.'

Poo and stinkbombs, I thought as I went back to my room. She'd have me going to the gig with a flask and cucumber sandwiches if she had her way. She really has no idea. And I'd really been looking forward to arriving at the gig on the back of a cool motorbike. The boys in the band would have been well impressed, but no, Mrs Killjoy had to have her way again. It's not fair. I met her halfway and brought Josh here and yet she still insists on treating me like a little girl who has to do as she says.

As soon as Mum dropped me off, I made a dive for the ladies, where I binned the sandwich she'd made me, reapplied my make-up and took off the top that I'd put on over the basque. Mum really didn't understand. I couldn't possibly get up on stage in front of everyone, looking like I was dressed for afternoon tea with my grandma.

When I came out, I saw that Spider had turned up and was standing with Josh at the bar, and my heart sank. He gave me his greeting sneer, and for the first time, I started to feel sympathy for the boy that Lucy had dumped for being too possessive. It's hard when you like someone but don't want to hang out with their friends or family, because people come as a package. It's like – like me, accept my mum. Like Josh, accept Spider.

Not long after, all my mates arrived – Nesta and Tony, TJ with Lucy's brothers, Steve and Lal, and of course, Lucy.

'Bring on the show,' Lucy said, grinning. 'Your fan club's here.'

I grinned back. 'Thanks.' It felt great to have them all there and made it feel more like a party than a performance in front of a strange audience.

I introduced Josh to everyone and he insisted on buying a round of drinks.

'What would you like, Izzie?' he asked.

'Pineapple,' I said. 'Need to keep a clear head for the performance.'

'A *drink* drink might take the edge off your nerves.'

'Maybe later,' I said. 'In the meantime, I have to remember my lyrics.'

The girls asked for Cokes, Josh and Spider ordered lager as usual, and when we'd all got our drinks, we stood at the back of the hall and listened to the first band. They were awful. Most of the time, I try to be supportive of fellow musicians, but even Ben caught my eye from the front of the hall and grimaced. Spider, however, wasn't as subtle and started heckling.

'Geddoff! Rubbish,' he called from the bar.

Josh laughed and went to get more drinks, but I didn't think it was funny. I thought it was really uncool. I moved away from Spider so that the musicians on stage wouldn't think that I was with him. Josh saw me frowning at Spider and when he brought me another drink, he said, 'Lighten up, Iz. They *are* rubbish. Better someone tells them so they don't waste any more of their time.'

'Give them a break. They're probably just starting out,' I said. 'I'm sure there was a time when even Robbie Williams sounded bad.'

'Doubt it,' said Josh, then took my chin in his hand, looked into my eyes and kissed me quickly. 'You, my dear Izzie, are far too nice.'

By this time, Spider had started looning about, doing mad dancing in the middle of the dance floor. Josh went to join him and soon people were looking at them and laughing instead of watching the band. I felt so sorry for them, as I know it takes courage to get up on stage.

'Looks familiar,' said Nesta, coming over. '*Please* tell me that I was never that embarrassing.'

'Ancient history,' I said. 'And at least you could dance.'

'And what about Josh? I thought he was ancient history.'

I shook my head. 'Nah. He's all right, really. He's got another side to him, once you get to know him. He's like a little boy who needs a bit of looking after.'

Nesta took a sip of my pineapple juice, then looked at me with surprise. 'Might be you who needs looking after if you have any more of these. I thought you weren't going to drink again after that night at my house.'

'What do you mean? It's only juice.'

'Yeah, right,' said Nesta. 'With a good measure of vodka in it.'

'Ohmigod,' I said. I'd had two large ones. I was so thirsty and didn't want my throat to be dry when I sang. No wonder I was feeling light-headed.

'Didn't you know?' asked Nesta

I shook my head.

'You need to watch it with him,' said Nesta. 'Slipping you drinks when you don't know isn't on.'

'No, really, he's OK. He was probably trying to loosen me up, as I told him how nervous I was.'

'That's your problem. You always see the best in people.'

'And that's yours. You always see the worst.'

Nesta looked at me with concern. 'No, seriously, Iz.

You take care with him. You might have forgotten that he left you stranded the other night, but I haven't.'

'But he apologised for that,' I said.

'And that makes it all right, does it?'

I didn't like the way the conversation was going. It felt like the great party atmosphere from earlier had become heavy. 'Look, Nesta, he's OK. You should give him a chance and get to know him. There are things going on in his life that you don't know about. Don't be so judgmental.'

Nesta looked hurt and I was about to apologise when Ben waved me over to get ready to go on stage.

'Catch you later,' said Nesta. 'Have a good one up there.'

I felt confused as I watched her walk back to Lucy and her brothers. What just happened there? I asked myself as I went for a last minute lipstick check in the ladies. TJ was in there combing her hair.

'You nervous?' she asked.

'Bit,' I said.

'And how's the stud?'

I lifted the basque and showed her. 'It's healed up nicely, see? I've been really good about keeping it clean and it seems to have worked OK.'

'Oh yeah. Looks great. But what about your mum? Did she ever find out you had another one put in?'

'Sort of,' I said. 'It's awkward. She read my diary. I know I put something about the new stud in there, but I think she feels bad about having read it – knows she shouldn't have – and it's been kind of unspoken since then. She knows, I know she knows, but neither of us wants to say anything.'

'Well, at least she hasn't told you to take it out again.'

'No. If she did, it would bring up the whole diary reading thing again and I guess she doesn't want to do that.'

'Yeah,' said TJ, slicking on some lip-gloss, then heading for the door. 'OK. Best of luck up there.'

'Thanks . . . Hey, TJ. What do you think of Josh?'

TJ hesitated. 'Oh, I can't say, Izzie. This is the first time I've met him and we've hardly said two words. I can see why you fancy him, but . . .'

'But what?'

'Well, I know Lucy and Nesta are a bit worried.'

'Why?'

TJ shrugged. 'It's probably nothing, but he's, well, he's not like the rest of us, is he? You can see he's got an edge.'

'So? I think that's what makes him so attractive.'

'I know. Just, Nesta thinks he may be a bad influence.'

Suddenly I felt really sad. So they've been talking about me behind my back, I thought. I hate that. I always think if you have anything to say, say it to the person in question. That's what being mates is all about . . . but then maybe I'm growing away from mine. It's felt kind of weird with us all lately.

★ ★ ★

King Noz did a twenty-minute set and the audience seemed to like it well enough. A few minutes into the first number, they were up and dancing away. I loved it. It's a real buzz being up on stage when the nerves disappear, the lights are on you and the music's rocking.

After I did my two numbers with the band, I went and sat with Josh and Spider.

Josh leaned back and gave me a wide grin. 'Impressive,' he said. 'You're hot.'

Spider gave me a kind of grudging smile. I think that meant he liked it as well. At least he didn't get up and heckle us.

As we sat to watch the rest of the set, Spider disappeared outside for a short while, then reappeared with a joint, which he handed to Josh then Josh passed to me. I quickly glanced to check that the barman wasn't looking as I didn't think teenagers smoking dope in the pub would go down too well, but he was busy serving customers. I noticed Nesta staring at me from the other side of the room. I gave her a wave, then purposely took a puff on the joint so she could see and inhaled like Josh had told me to do. If you think Josh is a bad influence, then I may as well let him be, I thought, as my head began to swim. I saw Nesta glance at TJ and TJ looked over at me and said something to Lucy. I took another puff on the joint and gave them a wave too.

I don't remember too much after that. Dancing with

Josh. Snogging Josh. Having a laugh with Josh. Falling asleep on his shoulder. The time went so quickly. The next thing I knew TJ was standing over me. 'Izzie. Lucy's mum's here to give you a lift home.'

'Oh, not yet,' said Josh as I got myself together to go. 'It's too early.'

'Curfew time,' I mumbled. 'Dragon Mother will be waiting.'

Josh laughed and walked with me to the car park where I could see Lucy talking to her mum, then glancing back at me. My God, I thought, who isn't talking about me? My head felt really thick and dopey and everyone seemed to be looking at me. Want to go home, I thought. Go to bed.

Mrs Lovering beckoned me over and Lucy squeezed in the back with Steve and Lal, while I took the front passenger seat. I closed my eyes and we drove for a while in silence.

'Tired, Izzie?' said Mrs Lovering.

'Um,' I replied.

'Good gig?'

'Excellent,' said Lal from the back. 'Izzie was a star.'

'So, you kids,' continued Mrs Lovering. 'I remember when I was your age . . .'

Ah, I thought, opening my eyes and turning to look at Lucy in the back. It's the 'When I was your age' speech. I knew Lucy had put her mum up to this. She shrugged, smiled weakly and stared out of the window, trying her best to look innocent.

'. . . it was quite a time,' continued Mrs Lovering. 'Go to a gig like that and everything would be on offer, and I don't mean just alcohol, know what I mean?'

'No,' I said, also trying to look innocent. 'What do you mean?'

'Oh, drugs. Pot, acid, coke . . .'

I had to laugh to myself. So, is that what everyone thinks now? Izzie's a raving junkie. I've only had a few puffs on a joint and now everyone's on my case.

'It can be hard to say no sometimes,' said Mrs Lovering. 'People can pressurise you to join in, even when you don't want to. All I'm saying is, be careful, guys. I know you're going to experiment and ultimately you have to make your own choices, but don't ever feel you have to do something because everyone else is. Right?'

'Right,' said Lucy from the back.

I turned around and gave her a cheesy smile. 'But Lucy's had Coke tonight, haven't you, Luce?'

'Coca-Cola,' said Lucy quickly.

For some reason, I thought this was hilarious and started giggling to myself, then I tried to make my face go straight. Boy, I do feel a bit weird, I thought, as I gazed out the window. A man at a bus stop gazed back. Not you too, I thought, as we whizzed by. I wish everyone would stop *looking* at me.

Parent Speak

Says:	Means:
When I was your age . . .	Prepare for a lecture about how when they were your age, they were a lot better behaved.
What's this lying on the floor?	It's yours. Pick it up immediately.
We need to have a 'word'.	Prepare for a telling-off
That TV programme doesn't look very interesting.	Turn it off.
It's getting late.	Go to bed
Your room's a mess.	Tidy it RIGHT NOW.
Are you watching this TV programme?	Turn over, I want to watch something else.
It's time you learned how to look after yourself as I won't be around forever.	Wash up.

Chapter 13

How Embarrassing!

When I was in Year Seven, I used to get a magazine that had a section in it with people's most embarrassing moments. People sent in all sorts of anecdotes about being caught naked, or a bee flying down their shorts, or pulling people's wigs off, and so on. I think I now qualify for the star prize.

I'd been home an hour, all snuggled up in my lovely bed after the gig, when my mobile rang. It was Josh.

'Want to live dangerously?' he said.

'Dunurrh . . .' I said sleepily.

'I'm outside. Meet me at the bottom of your road in five minutes.'

That woke me up fast enough. 'Out*side*? But it's midnight.'

'So? You going to turn into a pumpkin or what? Come

on, Iz. You start school again Monday. You can be a good girl then. Come on, come out and play.'

I wasn't feeling too good after the spiked pineapple juice and the joint earlier, and the thought of snuggling back down to sleep was very inviting. But so was sneaking out to be with Josh. I'd never done anything like that before. Why not? I thought. Everyone seems to think I'm bad. So why not live up to my reputation for once?

I pulled on my jeans and a fleece, grabbed my mobile and tiptoed out into the corridor, past Mum's room where I could hear Angus snoring, then down the stairs and into the front garden.

Josh was waiting for me at the gate. 'Excellent,' he said, putting his arm around me. 'Where shall we go?'

'Dunno,' I said.

'OK. I parked my bike at the end of the next road. I'll take us down to Queen's Wood.'

Five minutes later, I was clinging on to Josh's waist as we roared through the empty streets. It felt totally exhilarating and daring.

When we got to the park, we found a shelter near one of the gates and Josh produced a bottle of Malibu and a joint. 'Picnic,' he said.

'I wish,' I said. Apart from a piece of toast when I'd got in, I hadn't eaten since lunchtime. I suddenly realised I was starving. I shook my head when he offered me the bottle.

'No thanks. But you haven't by any chance got a cheese sandwich on you, have you?' I said, wishing I hadn't binned the one Mum had made me earlier. My stomach felt really peculiar.

Josh pouted. 'But I bought it specially for you,' he said, looking at the Malibu. 'It's not my thing. It's a chick's drink.'

I didn't want him to feel that I didn't appreciate the gesture so I took a swig. Then he offered me the joint.

'No thanks. I don't really like it,' I said.

'Give it another go,' he said. 'I don't want to get stoned on my own.' Then he looked away, his expression really sad. 'Dad's down the police station again. Don't know when he'll be back this time. I'm not ready to go home yet and I . . . I don't want to be on my own.'

Poor Josh, I thought. It must be awful having to stay out for fear of going home to bad news. I took the joint and had a quick puff, but this time, I tried not to inhale. It didn't seem to make much difference, though, as once again, my head began to feel woozy.

'Hmm . . . it's weird this, isn't it? Makes you feel funny.'

Josh smiled and pulled me close to him. 'Yeah, but funny in a cool way. You looked great tonight, did I tell you that?' He started kissing me, which felt really nice, then after a few minutes, I noticed his hands starting to stray from my back and around to my front.

I pushed him away.

'What's the matter?' he asked.

I felt confused. Ben had never tried this on with me and I didn't know what to do. Suddenly I was aware that I was in a park in the middle of the night and if Josh got annoyed, he could well abandon me again. Josh handed me the Malibu bottle. 'Here, have some more drink.'

'No, really,' I said. 'I don't want any.' My head was feeling thick again, my stomach was rumbling, I was cold and starting to feel a bit nauseous.

Josh moved in and started the wandering hands act again. Once more, I pushed him off. He sat back and handed me the bottle. 'Look, have a drink. Most girls find that it helps loosen them up.'

Well, I'm not most girls, I thought. But then I do like Josh, so maybe I should just go along with it and see what happens. I don't want him to think that I'm uptight, plus the drink might take my mind off the fact that I'm starving.

I took the bottle from him and had a good long glug.

'Good girl,' said Josh, snuggling up. 'It can help you chill out, that's all.' He started kissing me again and his hands started roaming around again. I could tell he was getting worked up because his breathing changed. It got heavier and his kisses got more urgent. At one point, he put his hand on my tummy.

'Oh, be careful,' I said. 'I've got a new stud.'

'Really?' he said and lifted up my fleece. 'Cool.'

And then it happened . . .

I threw up.

'Eeeeww!' he cried in surprise and sprang away.

I was horrified. I leaped up, ran for the gate and scrabbled around in my pockets for a tissue. I felt awful. My first encounter with a boy that goes a bit further than snogging and I *throw up*. It's never like this in the movies. I'll never live it down. I'm useless, I thought, as I ran out on to the pavement. My first drink and I fall asleep behind Nesta's sofa. My first cigarette and I gag on it. My first puff on a joint and I think everyone's watching me. And my first grope with a boy and I *puke!* How grown-up is that? Not at all. I felt close to tears and anything but fourteen. I felt like sitting on the pavement and crying like a baby.

All I wanted to do was get away. I went and stood at the bus stop, praying that a bus would come along so that I could get home, get into bed, wake up in the morning to find out it was all a bad dream.

'A bus has just gone,' said a lady going by with her dog.

Oh, now what? I thought as I looked around. The tube would be closed at this time. The streets were empty apart from the occasional car and the trees seemed alive somehow, shadowy, monstrous and threatening. I thought about going back to find Josh, but the woods looked so dense and dark. I didn't want to risk it.

A black Golf drove past filled with lads, then it reversed and slowly came back. 'Want a lift, darling?' called one.

I shook my head. 'My dad's coming to get me,' I said. Oh, where's Josh? I thought. Why hasn't he followed me? Oh God. What a disaster. He's probably trying to wipe off puke from his fleece where it splashed him. Luckily the boys in the car drove off and I sighed with relief. This is really, *really* stupid of me, I thought. A mad, *mad* mistake. There are stories every other week about girls my age disappearing, never to be seen again. I'm an idiot to have come out so late. I *never* do stuff like this normally. I'm not thinking straight with everything that's happened and the stupid Malibu and that stupid joint. It all kind of made everything feel unreal for a while, but it *is* real. It's past midnight, very dark and I'm out on the streets on my own. I wish Lucy was here, I thought. And TJ. And Nesta. They'll all be tucked up in their beds, like I should be, so no way can I call them so late. Dad? No, he'd take too long to get here from Primrose Hill and I don't want to stay out on my own a moment longer than necessary. Then I thought about Mum asleep at home, thinking that I was safe in my room nextdoor to her. I want my mum, I thought. I wish she'd just drive by and pick me up. I don't want to be grown-up any more. I want to be looked after. Should I phone her? I asked myself. No. No way I can call her. I'll be grounded for a decade and never see daylight again. She'd go ballistic and she's got good reason, I said to myself as another car drove by and the male driver looked out at me. What on earth am I doing out here in the middle of the night on my own?

Chapter 14

Damsel in Distress

There was only one person to turn to and luckily he was still awake when I called. He only lived up the road and said he'd come straight out on his bicycle to get me. While I was waiting for him, Josh phoned my mobile and said that he was looking for me but wasn't sure which way I'd gone when I ran out of the park. I said I was sorry for throwing up and told him to go home as I was all right.

Twenty minutes later, I was curled up safely on the sofa in Ben's garage with a cup of tea and three rounds of Marmite toast.

'Thanks,' I said as I brushed the crumbs away from my mouth. 'I was starving. I missed supper and only had a snack when I got it after the gig.'

Ben grinned. 'More like a classic case of the munchies.

It often happens when people smoke dope.'

'Have you smoked it?'

Ben shrugged. 'Gave it a go. Not my scene, though, really. I prefer to have a clear head.'

I was surprised, as he'd never mentioned it before and I thought I knew all about him. Plus he didn't seem the type.

'I didn't like it very much,' I said. 'Made my head feel very thick, and back at the gig, it had a weird effect on me, like everyone was watching me. And later, in the park, even the *trees* seemed to be watching me.'

'Yeah, well, on an almost empty stomach, the effects would be amplified. No wonder you felt strange. Plus, there are different types of dope and they have different effects. Some can be quite hallucinogenic and make you feel like you're seeing things, other types just make you sleepy. Plus it's different for everyone. Some people it disagrees with. Take ecstasy, for example. Some people take just one tablet and it kills them, others seem to be fine. Hell of a risk, though. It's still early days, and researchers are still looking into its long term effects on the brain. Personally, I'd rather stay clear and not take any chances . . . And drink, that affects people differently as well. Some people get all happy when they've had too much to drink, others depressed and melancholic, others get aggressive and argumentative, others just throw up. I guess it depends on your body chemistry.'

'Yeah. My stepmother Anna is really funny when she's been drinking. Something seems to happen to the volume control on her voice. She starts talking *really* loud but doesn't realise it.'

'So, what's been with you lately, trying all this stuff? I thought you were Miss Straight White and Bright. You know, well into health foods . . .'

'I know. I was. I am. I just wanted to try something different. Part of it was wanting to be more grown-up, more sophisticated.'

Ben started laughing. 'And doing the technicolour yawn all over Josh was part of that, was it?'

'Not quite all over him, but I think I did get him a bit. I've never been so embarrassed in all my life. I doubt if I'll see him again.'

'Maybe you will. Maybe you won't. But throwing up over someone is an interesting seduction tactic. Er, not one I'd try again, though.'

Now that I was safe, fed and warm, I started to see the funny side. 'Well, magazines are always telling us that when starting a new relationship, it's good to let someone see the inside of you that you don't show the rest of the world.'

Ben laughed again. 'Yeah, but I don't think they meant literally, as in what you ate that day. At least he'll never forget you.'

'Yeah. Oh God, Ben. It's been such a weird time lately. All I wanted was for people to take me seriously and treat me like an adult and I seem to have done nothing but act like a right twerp.'

'I don't think that being grown-up means that you have to smoke or drink or anything,' said Ben. 'I think that being grown-up means finding out what you want as an individual and having the voice to say so, regardless of what anyone else thinks. Loads of fakers at our school drink and smoke because they think it looks cool. To me, that's not what being cool is about. Being cool is being true to yourself.'

'It's hard to say no sometimes, though.'

'Why?'

'Dunno. It's like you feel pressurised to do stuff or try new experiences. Like tonight in the park, I didn't want to seem like a baby, you know, doing stuff for the first time. And I didn't want to refuse Josh's offer of drink for fear of offending him. And then, well, later, I didn't want to come across as uptight.'

'You're too nice, Izzie.'

'That's what Josh said.'

'There will always be people you'll offend. What's that saying? You can't please all the people all of the time. Never go along with a guy just because you're afraid of offending him. You have feelings too. What do *you* want? You can't make everyone like you, Iz. And you shouldn't try to be someone you're not just to please a boy. If you do, you'll lose yourself. Just be who you are. Don't do stuff with a guy unless you really want to and the time is right. If a guy's the one for you, he'll take you at the pace you want to go.'

'Ever thought of being an agony aunt, Ben?

He smiled and put his arm around me. 'Auntie Ben. Yeah, if the music doesn't turn out maybe I'll go for a new career.'

It felt so comforting to sit there snuggled up to him for a while. No pressure, no stress. If you had to pick an animal to represent how others see you, Ben, I thought, you should pick a big old sheepdog. Cuddly, safe and warm.

At that moment, we heard a car pull up outside.

Ben looked out of the window. 'Taxi's here,' he said.

Ben walked me out and saw me into the cab. 'Here's a tenner,' he said. 'Should be enough. Got your keys?'

I nodded. 'And hopefully Mum and Angus will still be happily in dreamland.' I gave him a hug. 'Thanks, Ben. You've been a real mate.'

'Talking of which,' he said. 'Get together with yours. They're a good lot and when you're out, it's important that you all stick together, look after one another, make sure you all get home safe. And never leave each other alone with boys that you don't know well.'

I pinched his arm. 'Since when did you get so grown-up?'

He smiled back. 'Since you started acting like a five-year-old.'

Song for Ben
Knight on a Battered Bicycle

I was distressed,
In a real mess,
Cast down,
Lost my crown,
No more a princess.

I cried out for rescue and look what came my way.

You're my knight in crumpled armour,
My hero for a day.
Forget the milk-white charger,
You just peddle up my way.

I cried for help and look what came my way.

Wheels of fire and thunder
Are OK for the Gods,
But a crossbar lift is just the thing
To hold back all my sobs.

Ring your bell and wheel my way,
My knight in crumpled armour.
Ring your bell and wheel my way,
My knight in crumpled armour.

Chapter 15

Ground Rules

Sunday was Mum's birthday and Angus had insisted that she have a lie-in as a treat. I went down to the kitchen and prepared a tray – a cafetière of coffee, orange juice, toast and the chunky marmalade that she likes. Then I cut a rose from the fence in the back garden and put it in a small vase next to my card and present for her.

Angus was already up and pottering in his study. 'That looks nice,' he said as I went past.

'It's for Mum.'

'Good for you.' He smiled. 'She's probably ready for a cup of coffee now.'

Mum was still dozing when I tiptoed into her room. I watched her sleeping for a few moments and felt really warm towards her. She looked so young and vulnerable somehow, lying there with her hair splayed on the pillow, one arm thrown above her head. Did you ever stay out at night and misbehave? I wondered. Somehow I couldn't imagine it. She's always so efficient, organised and controlled. A typical Virgo, according to my astrology book.

She opened her eyes as I put the tray on the bedside cabinet, then got up and sat on the edge of the bed.

'Is that for me?' she said, rubbing her eyes.

I nodded. 'Happy birthday.'

'Oh Izzie, how lovely. Thank you. And a present.'

I watched as she opened her card and present.

'Oils for the bath,' she said, taking the lid off one of the bottles and sniffing. 'Mmm. Lovely.'

'It's got lavender and rosewood in it — aromatherapy oils. They're supposed to be good for relaxation.'

'It smells divine, Izzie. Thank you so much.'

'And . . . and I wanted to say I'm sorry I've been a pain lately and that I really do appreciate you as a mother.'

She laughed. 'OK, what have you done now?'

'*Nothing*,' I said. Luckily, I'd managed to sneak back in last night without waking her and Angus. What she doesn't know won't hurt her, I thought. 'Mum?'

'What?'

'What were you like when you were my age?'

Mum laughed. 'Pretty timid, really.'

'Did you ever do anything stupid?'

'What, like you at Nesta's the other night?'

'Yes. No. I mean, didn't you used to experiment with, I don't know, cigarettes? The occasional drink?'

'Not really,' she said. 'Let me think. I did try a cigarette once, but hated it. As you know, I've never smoked. Drink . . . When did I have my first drink? I didn't really drink until I was at university and then not a lot. Couldn't afford it on my student's grant. Oh dear. Am I a terrible disappointment? Boring? I'm afraid I was never one for experimenting much and there wasn't as much on offer out there, or at least not that I was aware of. My parents were so strict with me, and to tell you the truth, when I did finally leave home and go to college, I thought I'd lived a sheltered life compared to the rest of them. I was a bit of a late developer, really. That's why . . . I look at you and you're *so* different to how I was – I suppose that's why I fear for you. My endlessly curious Izzie. You were always the same, from the moment you were born. Into everything. Restless. Always asking questions. We may be mother and daughter and have some similar features – eyes, the shape of our hands . . . but your spirit is your own and as opposite to mine as it could ever be. And now, so grown-up, still curious, and yet . . . I don't know. I can't help but worry about you and what's out there. For one thing, the streets felt a lot safer when I was young. I thought nothing about walking home on my own at night. These days, I'd never let you do that.'

Tell me about it, I thought. Last night is not an experience I want to repeat in a hurry. 'Well, it's nice to have someone worry about you,' I said.

Mum smiled. 'I can't help it. And I know I overreact sometimes, but it's only because I care. I know that there are drugs in school and a lot of teenagers smoke and drink. It's just I want you to enjoy your adolescence, enjoy being young, and yet you're so busy wanting to grow up and leave it all behind you. And boys . . . I . . . I worry that in wanting to grow up, you're going to feel pressurised to rush into things before you're ready. Just promise me that you'll be careful, whatever happens.'

'I will and I'm OK, Mum. Honest. And I'm learning. Yes, it is mad out there. And yes, you can feel pressurised, but I think I know when to say no or yes. Or whatever.'

'And . . . um, how's your stud? Has it healed up?'

I laughed. At last, she'd acknowledged that she knew about it. 'Yeah, it's good now. But . . . er, how did you know about that?'

She grinned. 'You know very well. Your diary, of course. I *am* sorry about that, Izzie. It was wrong of me. I should have respected your privacy. But you know what? No one gives you a rule book on how to be a teenager, and, well, no one gives you a rule book on how to be a mother either. And reading your diary was a mad mistake.'

I smiled back at her. 'We all make mad mistakes, Mum.'

'I know,' she said wistfully. 'But do you think in the future, we could, well, try and talk about them a bit more? You know, help each other.'

'Sure,' I said. 'I'm game for that. Want to see my stud?'

'If I must,' she said, then she pulled a silly face.

'So, does this mean you're back with Ben now?' asked Nesta later that morning.

Straight after I'd taken Mum her breakfast, I'd called TJ, Lucy and Nesta and asked them to come over. Luckily they were all free, and by twelve o'clock we were all in my bedroom, where I told them about what had happened last night.

I shook my head. 'No, I'm not getting back with him, but we are best mates. Like you lot.'

Nesta and TJ looked at each other, while Lucy stared at the carpet.

'Because we *are* best mates, aren't we?' I asked.

'Course,' said Lucy. 'We have bonded for life over the Almighty Pringle, remember?'

'Maybe we should have done the finger pricking thing,' I said. 'Done it properly.'

'Oh *please*, don't start that again,' moaned Nesta.

'Don't worry,' I reassured her. 'I won't. But I did want to see you all today and say I'm sorry. I guess I've been a bit distant lately and acting a bit out of character. But last night, it made me realise that you guys are the most important people in my life. Besides Mum and Dad, of course . . . and . . . and Angus. It's weird – like, remember how I used to hate him and call him The Lodger? Well, he's been cool lately and I'm starting to really like him. So yeah, Angus is important too.'

'Well, we've been worried about you, Iz,' said Lucy. 'It was like you didn't want to be associated with us any more. You used to phone or e-mail every day, but this last week, I've hardly heard from you. Like you'd moved on and thought we were too childish for you or something.'

'No way,' I said.

'Last night, you hardly spent any time with us,' said Nesta. 'We all thought you were ashamed of us or something, because we didn't want to drink and smoke and be in with your new crowd.'

'*Ashamed* of you? I thought *you* didn't want to be with me and you didn't like Josh or Spider.'

'Didn't like Spider. He's kind of creepy,' said Nesta.

'Maybe that's why his nickname is Spider,' said TJ. 'Creepy crawly. So what about Josh? Are you going to see him again?'

'Doubt it somehow,' I said. 'I think throwing up just as he was getting snuggly was probably a bit of a turn-off, don't you think?'

'Dunno,' laughed TJ. 'But you could probably make it work if you wanted. Phone him up and apologise, and so on.'

'Nah. Think I'll give him a break for a while. It's kind of done my head in this last week. Part of me felt sorry for him because he's not happy at home. I thought I could make it better, I guess. I thought I could change him, but . . .'

'As you told me your mum said once, the only time you can change a man is when he's a baby,' said Lucy.

'Exactly,' I said. 'It was exciting being with him, but also exhausting. I didn't feel like I could totally be myself. I was trying to be something different for him.'

'So why not go back with Ben?'

'Dunno. It's like, being with Ben was safe and secure and Josh was the total opposite, unpredictable and exciting. Maybe there are some boys who are a bit of both. Do you think?'

'I think my brother's a bit like that,' said Nesta. 'Don't you think, Lucy?'

Lucy blushed. 'Yeah. He's pretty cool. And my brothers are a bit of each. Lal is pretty mad, whereas Steve is pretty sensible.'

'Yes, but he's not boring sensible,' said TJ. 'And he can be mad sometimes.'

I looked around at the three of them and sighed with relief. It felt good. We were talking again.

'You know what?' I said. 'I really *really* don't want to lose you guys as friends. I'm sorry if I've been acting like a prize prat. I don't know what came over me.'

'Maybe it's because we'll all be going into Year Ten tomorrow,' said Lucy. 'Makes you think about the next chapter. Like where are we going next.'

'Yeah. It's going to be weird being back at school,' said TJ. 'It's like, in the holidays, all the days just flow into each other. No Monday, Tuesday, Wednesday, weekend and so on. When we're at school, the whole week is punctuated. Sunday night, get ready for school. Monday, go to school. Wait for Friday. Then the weekend.'

'I know what you mean,' I said. 'Back to the old routine after a mad, mad summer.'

'How's things with your mum?' asked TJ.

'Better,' I said. 'I mean, she'll never be cool like your mum, Lucy. She'll always be straight, but that's who she is. We had a good talk this morning and she's even OK about me having my stud now.'

'Yeah, but you really started something, Izzie,' said Lucy. 'I think it was because of last night when Mum drove us home. She was a bit concerned about you, then started asking if I ever smoked or drank. You know, the whole interrogation. This morning at breakfast, she said she wanted to "have a talk". It was so embarrassing. One of those "Let's talk openly about things" type talks. Steve and Lal looked like they wanted to die.'

'Have a talk about what?' said TJ.

'First, drink – how when you drink, you're not always in control of your thoughts or actions and must be careful not to be in the wrong place or somewhere unfamiliar. Then how smoking wrecks your skin . . .'

'I think it does,' I said. 'I've got two aunts – one has smoked all her life, the other never has. The one who smokes is ten years younger than the other one, yet looks ten years older. Her skin is sort of crêpey and dried out.'

'Well,' continued Lucy, 'then we got how drinking can wreck your liver. As if we're going to be drinking bottles of the stuff . . .'

'Yeah,' I said. 'If I've learned anything these holidays, it's about balance. All things in moderation and not to go overboard like I did at yours that night, Nesta . . .'

'But the main thing she said about drink and drugs,' Lucy said, 'is that both can alter your perception. She said her anxiety was that one of us would be out of our heads and not thinking straight and someone would take advantage. A boy or someone, when we didn't know what we were doing. She kept saying that your facility to make proper choices gets impaired, but I think that's only if you drink too much.'

I thought back to last night. 'That was exactly what Josh wanted,' I said. 'Me to get drunk so that he could have a jolly old grope.'

Nesta shook her head. 'Not on,' she said. 'Not my romantic fantasy, anyway. If you have to get totally plastered to get it on with a boy, then it can't be right, can it? I'd want to be sure that I wanted to do it sober *or* having had a drink. It's like, if you have to get out of your head to do it, maybe you're trying to get out of the situation on some level. It can't be what you really want to do.'

'And then Mum started on about drugs,' Lucy continued. 'She said that one of the biggest risks is that sometimes stuff gets mixed in with them and people don't know what they're actually taking. Unless you know exactly where the drugs have come from, they could be laced with anything.'

'Well, at least she didn't give you the sex lecture,' I said. 'That can be really embarrassing.'

'Oh, don't worry, I got that one,' said TJ. 'Sometimes it's hard having doctors as parents, as they see the down-side of everything and think they have to pass it all on. I got a lecture about sexually transmitted diseases and the number of teenage pregnancies my mum sees. She said everyone thinks it can't happen to them and some of the girls she sees are our age and got pregnant the very first time they had sex.'

I remembered what Ben had said last night, about never going along with a boy for fear of hurting his feelings. I wondered if some of the girls who got pregnant simply got into a situation and didn't know how to get out of it – didn't have the courage to say that they weren't ready. Or got so drunk, they didn't realise how far they were going until it was too late, or so drunk that they didn't even care about the risks.

'You know what, girls?' I said. 'Back to school tomorrow, and as TJ said, it's a new start. We don't know what we're going to encounter, and what boys are on the horizon for the next year. Or what any of us are going to go through. I reckon we need to make some ground rules to mark our Pringle bonding. It wasn't enough to eat a bite of it and think we'd be bonded for life . . .'

'Oh no . . .' said Nesta. 'What are you going to make us do now?'

'Nothing bad. It's just, there are times when maybe we need to watch out for each other. I think we should think about what we really need from each other when there are boys around or drink or drugs, or whatever. How about we all write down a ground rule? Fold it up and put in a hat. I'll do a printout of them on my computer for us all to keep.'

'Good idea,' said Nesta. 'Rule One: no having to prick your thumb in order to be mates.'

I punched her arm. 'Yeah, that and a few others.'

Ground Rules for Mates

- Remember: trying to change or save a boy is a lost cause. The only time you can change a boy is when he's a baby.
- If you're going to experiment with anything, whatever it is, make sure you know where it's come from. And do it somewhere safe with someone you trust. Drugs *and* drink can be laced.
- If one of us gets off with a boy the rest of us don't know, the others must keep an eye out for where we are.
- Always make sure *all* of us have got a lift home or are travelling home together.
- Keep talking to each other, even if one of us has gone a bit weird.

Chapter 16

Police

Later in the afternoon, we went up to Muswell Hill to buy some special card for printing our ground rules on to. Halfway down the Broadway, who should we see standing outside Marks and Spencer, but Josh.

Nesta nudged me. 'Eyes right,' she said. 'Trouble ahead.'

Josh hadn't seen me, and for a moment, I felt like turning around and running. But no, I told myself, be grown-up about this. I can't spend my life running away from boys I've had a bad time with.

'Do you want us to come with you?' asked TJ.

I shook my head. 'Nah, just give me a minute.'

The girls headed into a nick-nack shop next to Marks and Spencer and I took a deep breath and walked over to Josh. He looked very surprised to see me, like a rabbit caught in the headlights.

I smiled. 'Hey, Josh.'

He looked up and down the road as though he wanted to make a getaway.

'I wasn't *that* bad, was I?' I said, trying to make a joke of last night.

'Nah, course not,' he said, nervously glancing into Marks and Spencer as though looking for someone.

'Are you all right?' I asked.

Just at that moment, I saw a policeman come out of the shop. He took one look at Josh and headed straight for him. Now Josh really did look uncomfortable. He stared at the pavement, like he was hoping it would open up and swallow him whole. I glanced over at the policeman. No doubt about it, he was definitely coming for Josh. Hell's bells, I thought, as my mind began to run riot. Josh is in trouble. Maybe he's been caught smoking dope in the park. Oh God, he's going to be arrested. I started to panic inside. Oh no, what if it gets back to Mum, just when I've made it up with her. It will ruin everything.

The policeman stopped, turned to look at me and smiled a really friendly smile. Uh? I thought. What's going on?

'Well, come on, then, Josh,' said the policeman. 'Introduce us.'

Josh sighed heavily. 'Um, this is Izzie,' he muttered. 'Izzie, this is . . . this is . . . my dad.'

Josh's *dad*! I thought. His dad is a *policeman*?

Josh's dad beamed at me. 'So you're Izzie? You're the one Josh went to see sing last night. Good to meet you.'

My brain went into overdrive. A policeman? Of course. Oh poo. I've been so *stupid*. 'Dad spends a lot of time down at the police station,' Josh had said. 'Never know where he is . . .'. I'd just assumed that his dad was a criminal and he'd let me believe it. I could kick myself. Stupid, stupid, I thought. It was all coming back to me. Josh saying how easy it was to feed girls a line, then they just run with it, hear what they want to hear. Exactly what I'd done, and when he'd seen I'd fallen for it, hook, line and sinker, he hadn't done anything to disillusion me. Of *course*, a boy like Josh *would* say that he didn't want to end up like his dad. And he never actually said the word 'criminal'.

'Um, yeah. Izzie,' I blustered. Close up, Josh's dad looked really nice. Big and jolly. Nothing like the difficult man who had no time for his son, who Josh had described.

'Josh never lets me or his mum meet his friends,' he continued, 'so it's good to see one of you at last. Come over to the house one day – that is, if you can get Josh to bring you. He's never at home these days. We never see him. I hope you're not like that with your parents.'

I glanced at Josh. He was still staring at the pavement, looking like he wanted to die.

Later, we all went back to Lucy's for a farewell-to-the-holiday pizza. The girls thought it was hysterical when I told them what had happened.

'We were watching from inside the shop,' said Lucy. 'We thought you were going to be arrested.'

'I know. So did I for a moment. Even though I haven't done anything wrong, the minute he started walking towards me, I felt so guilty.'

'Until he turned out to be Josh's dad,' laughed Nesta.

'I know, I could have kicked myself! Talk about gullible, that's me. Just called me stupid.'

'No,' said TJ. 'It could have happened to any of us.'

'Well, never again,' I said. 'I'm older, wiser, smarter.'

'Until next time,' said Nesta. 'Some guy will come along, flutter his eyelashes, and . . .'

'Maybe,' I said, 'but I don't think I'll be quite as gullible next time.'

Once we'd finished the pizza, I got ready to go.

'You're leaving early, Iz,' said Lucy.

'Ah well. This is the new sensible Izzie. School tomorrow, so I want to get my things ready, plus I said I'd look in on Mum's dinner party. You know it's her birthday today? Well, she's having some friends over. I'll only pop in for a minute or so, just to show my face as they'll probably all be sitting round, having some boring discussion about mortgages or something. Best show willing.'

'Hmm, sounds like a real fun time. Not,' said Nesta.

When I opened the front door at home, the strangest sight met my eyes. The kitchen was a total mess, and when I went and stuck my head round the living room door, I saw that all Mum's friends were up hippie dancing. They looked more than a bit merry, especially Angus who waved at me happily from the corner of the room. I stood in the doorway for a moment and watched with amazement. Mum saw me looking and came over. 'Do you want to join us, Izzie? Have half a glass of wine?'

'No thanks,' I said, then smiled. 'I've just got back from my AA meeting. I've gone teetotal.'

One of her friends looked at me oddly. 'Only joking,' I said, then headed up the stairs. I knew exactly what I was going to do. Bath, bed and a hot chocolate.

While the adults downstairs danced away, reliving their youth, I was happy to have an early night, tucked up like an old grandmother. Does anyone ever act their age? I wondered as the sounds of the Rolling Stones floated up through the ceiling. I thought about banging on the ceiling and asking them to turn the music down, then I thought no, Mum's only middle-aged once. I'll let her have her fun.

Song for Ageing Parents
C'mon Let's Dance

My mother is a hippie,

My stepdad is a geek,

My friends all play video games seven days a week.

I'm stuck in the middle, what else can I say?

We're all just little kids, though some of us are grey.

So let's dance, c'mon everybody, let's dance.

You're a short time growing up

And a very long time dead

Sometimes you gotta shake the serious

Right outta your head.

So let's dance, c'mon everybody, let's dance.

You're a short time growing up

And a very long time dead

So let's all shake the serious stuff

Right outta our heads.

Let's dance, c'mon everybody, let's dance.

So grab yourself a hippie, hang on to a freak.

Put your loudest music on and get up on your feet.

And let's dance, c'mon everybody, let's dance.

Let's dance, c'mon everybody, let's dance.

Cathy Hopkins

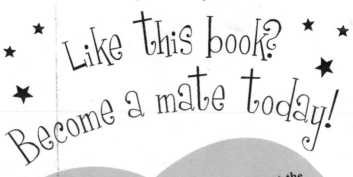

Like this book?

Become a mate today!

Join **CATHY'S CLUB** and be the first to get the lowdown on the LATEST NEWS, BOOKS and FAB COMPETITIONS straight to your mobile and e-mail.

PLUS there's a FREE MOBILE WALLPAPER when you sign up! What are you waiting for?

Simply text MATE plus your date of birth (ddmmyyyy) to 60022 now! Or go to www.cathyhopkins.com and sign up online.

Once you've signed up keep your eyes peeled for exclusive chapter previews, cool downloads, freebies and heaps more fun stuff all coming your way.

Texts to Cathy cost your normal rate/ texts from Cathy are free/ to unsubscribe at any time text STOP to 60022